ROSCOE

A CHRISTIAN ROMANTIC SUSPENSE

OATH OF HONOR

LAURA SCOTT

Copyright © 2024 by Laura Scott

All rights reserved.

No part of this book may be reproduced in any form or by any electronic or mechanical means, including information storage and retrieval systems, without written permission from the author, except for the use of brief quotations in a book review.

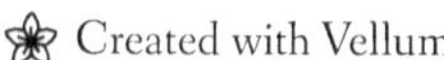 Created with Vellum

Libby Hall gripped the steering wheel tightly, growing concerned that the black truck two car lengths behind her was following her. Had been since she'd left the fleabag motel outside of Bloomington, Illinois.

Swallowing hard, she took note of the sign. Milwaukee, Wisconsin, was only ten miles away. Ten long miles until she reached Roscoe Turner. She took a deep breath and glanced down at her pregnant belly. "Soon, little one. We'll be safe soon."

Or so she hoped. Maybe she should have called Roscoe rather than making the long and impulsive drive from Texas. But finding her apartment ransacked with a huge knife stuck in the middle of her kitchen table had rattled her.

Badly.

Roscoe had mentioned his cousin Cameron lived in Milwaukee. She'd known Roscoe had left Texas after their huge fight; he was the one who helped arrest her brother in the first place. Using her to get to Tony. It had hurt that

Roscoe had kept his role as a cop secret. Especially after they spent the night together.

Now here she was, tracking down his cousin, hoping Cameron would tell her where to find Roscoe.

She tried not to think about how she'd cried on Roscoe's shoulder after getting the news her father had died of a heart attack. How she'd spent the night with him, only to discover almost a week later that Tony, had been arrested thanks to Roscoe using her to get key information to put her brother away for the rest of his life. Yes, her brother was a criminal; she didn't condone that behavior. But Tony had agreed to cooperate with the DEA to give up the cartel.

Glancing in the rearview mirror and seeing that the black truck was still two cars back, she realized the cartel must have been involved in searching her apartment. That maybe they had come after her out of revenge, sending a loud message to anyone else who dared to testify against them.

Please, Lord, keep us safe in Your care!

This was Roscoe's fault.

No, that wasn't fair. Tony, had been the one to transport drugs across the border. He'd done this. All Roscoe had done was to try to put a stop to it. And she couldn't blame him for that.

She could blame him for the way he'd gone about it. Making her believe he cared about her.

Letting her fall in love with him.

She carefully switched lanes, noting with a nauseating feeling of despair that the black truck followed suit. Glancing at her map app on her phone, she noted her exit was coming up. She waited until the last possible minute to get off the interstate, hoping the black truck would keep going. She turned right at the end of the ramp, then stomped on the gas to pick up speed.

The black truck was no longer behind her. Had she lost him?

She made another quick turn, then searched the street addresses. It helped that Cameron Stevenson's place wasn't too far from the interstate. She drove past the Wisconsin State Fair grounds, then turned left at the next cross street.

She pulled into the driveway, taking note of the squad sitting in the driveway. Was Cameron a cop too? Or was Roscoe there? She prayed it was the latter as she quickly slid out from behind the wheel, grabbed her purse, and hurried up to the front door.

Leaning on the doorbell, she cast a furtive glance behind her. So far, the street was clear.

It seemed to take an inordinate length of time for the front door to open. Her eyes widened when she saw Roscoe standing there.

"Libby?" He looked confused, then his gaze dropped to her pregnant belly. His eyes bulged with shock. "What in the—you'all are *pregnant?*"

"Surprise." She winced at her snarky tone. "But worse, I'm in danger. Someone wrecked my apartment, leaving a large knife embedded in my table. I'm afraid the cartel is responsible." Now that she was there, she was hit by an overwhelming feeling of relief. "I came here because I need your help . . ."

His gaze narrowed on something behind her. She turned in time to see the black truck rolling down the street, the passenger window open revealing a dark-skinned man. Certain the vehicle was the same one that had followed her from the Wisconsin-Illinois border, she instinctively ducked and darted away from the door just as the guy opened fire.

"Libby!" Roscoe flung the door open and stepped out holding his weapon with one hand. He fired at the retreating truck. She heard the metallic ping of the bullet striking the vehicle. Lifting her head, she saw the truck was still moving but faster now as the driver tried to evade them.

"Get inside!" Roscoe leaned down and grabbed her arm. She didn't need to be told twice. She stumbled into the house, shivering despite the warm July sun. Roscoe was dressed in casual clothes, jeans and a T-shirt, which made her think he had the day off. But if that was the case, why was the squad in the driveway? "Who was that? What's going on?" he demanded.

"I—don't know." Tears pricked her eyes, and she tried to pull herself together. "I think that truck has been following me since I left the motel."

"What motel?" Roscoe stared at her, then waved his hand. "Never mind. We need to get you out of here before they come back for a second round."

"First, I have to use the bathroom." The baby had been sitting on her bladder for the last twenty miles.

He looked like he might argue, then waved toward the hallway. "Go ahead. I'll call this in."

She hurried down the hall, listening as he made the call to report gunfire at this address. She was relieved to find Roscoe here, although she wasn't sure where Cameron was. Did the two guys share the house?

She told herself it didn't matter. She was here because Roscoe had started this nightmare by arresting her brother. By making the cartel angry enough to lash out at anyone associated with Tony.

Despite how much she detested what Roscoe had done, using her to get to her brother, she needed him to keep her and their baby safe.

It was the least he could do.

———

LIBBY HALL IS *pregnant with my child. And someone just tried to kill her.*

Roscoe filled the local law enforcement in on the recent shooting. Then he called his boss, Captain Rhyland Finnegan of the Milwaukee Police Department Tactical Team. "I need a couple of days off starting now."

"Okay," Rhy said after a long moment. "What's going on?"

He sighed, running his hand through his thick hair. "An old friend of mine showed up at the house, and someone tried to kill her."

"Did you call it in?" Rhy asked.

"Of course. But we can't stay here. I need to get her someplace safe." He was still reeling over Libby's unexpected arrival. "She's pregnant."

"Yours?"

"Yeah." He could take a paternity test, but the timing was right. Besides, Libby wasn't the type to sleep around. They—he shouldn't have taken advantage of her that night she'd learned her father had died. Pushing aside the guilt and shame, he focused on the present. "I'm more concerned with keeping her safe."

"Understood. You can try heading to the American Lodge, but it may be booked this close to the Fourth of July. You may need to go farther out to find a room."

He hadn't considered the timing related to the holiday. "Good point. In the meantime, I hope you don't hold this time off against me."

"You know me better than that," Rhy chided. "Family first."

Family. The word was like a sucker punch to the gut. Roscoe's cousin Cameron was the only family he had left after losing his adoptive parents. And while he and Cam were close now, they hadn't met until they were teenagers because their mothers were estranged. He liked Cam but was keenly aware that there was no blood bond between them.

Libby's baby proved he had a family now. No matter how things worked out for him and Libby, he would not abandon his child.

"Thanks, Rhy." He lowered the phone as Libby emerged from the bathroom. She looked as beautiful as always, despite the fear darkening her green eyes. Before he could say anything more, the wail of sirens filled the air. He raised his voice to be heard over the noise. "Please sit down and wait here. I need to talk to these officers before we head out."

She nodded, sinking into the closest chair and clutching her purse like a lifeline. He had so many questions, but right now, he needed to stay focused on finding these gunmen.

He strode to the door and watched as two local squads pulled up. Glancing back at Libby, he offered a reassuring smile as he headed outside to meet them.

"Officer Roscoe Turner from MPD," he said, showing his badge. "An extended cab Chevy truck drove past and fired two rounds at my—ah, Libby Hall." He'd stumbled over how to introduce Libby. She wasn't exactly his girlfriend any longer, although they had been close.

Until she'd learned he'd arrested her brother, Tony, for running drugs.

"License plate?" Officer Golden asked.

"No, it was partially covered in mud." Not to mention the whole thing had gone down too fast for him to get more than a passing glimpse. He turned to look at Cameron's house. "Here"—he pointed to the small round bullet holes in the siding—"these are the two slugs."

"We'll get them out and examined for markings," the second officer, by the name of Avery, replied.

The slugs were in the exact location Libby had been standing before she'd ducked to avoid them. The near miss made his blood run cold.

"We'd like to speak to Ms. Hall," Golden said.

"Sure." He led the way inside where Libby was still seated on the sofa. Seeing them, she struggled to her feet. He quickly crossed over to offer a hand. "Libby, Officer Golden and Officer Avery would like to ask you a few questions."

She looked at the cops warily. "I'm not sure I can be much help. I noticed the black truck keeping pace behind me after I left my motel earlier this morning. I, uh, came to Wisconsin to find Roscoe—er, Officer Turner. I, uh . . ." She floundered for a moment, then said, "My brother, Tony Hall, is in a federal prison for drug trafficking. He had once been working with one of the Mexican cartels."

Golden whistled. "I wouldn't want to mess with the cartels."

The color drained from Libby's face. "I was told Tony cooperated with the DEA for a lighter sentence. He's been in prison for about six months. Two days ago, when I came home from work, I found my apartment totally ransacked, and worse, a large knife was sticking out of the kitchen table." She bit her lower lip for a moment, pulling herself together before continuing. "I'm a teacher. I knew this had to be related to my brother. Fearing for my life and that of my child, I jumped in the car and drove away."

Roscoe felt sick knowing that his arresting Tony had put Libby and their baby in danger. Worse, she'd had her apartment trashed, then had been forced to drive for two days straight to get here. He should have stayed in Texas.

He should have been there for her all this time.

The two officers glanced at each other with concern. Golden asked, "You believe one of the Mexican cartels has followed you all the way here?"

"It's the only thing that makes sense." Libby sniffed and swiped at her damp eyes. "But I didn't notice the black car following me until I reached the Wisconsin state line." She shivered despite the warmth. "I guess I could have missed a tail after leaving Texas, but I was paying attention. Especially knowing someone had left a huge knife in my apartment." She swallowed hard and glanced at him. "I'm glad you were here. If you hadn't answered the door . . ."

"I'm glad I was here too." He ached to take her into his arms but couldn't seem to bring himself to close the gap between them. She had only sought him out now because of the danger.

Not because she was desperate to see him. In fact, he wasn't sure he'd have learned about the baby if her apartment hadn't been broken into.

His stomach tightened with guilt, anger, and frustration with both the situation and his own role in it. What had happened back in Texas? Was Tony still alive? In his experience, snitches were often killed in prison. But sometimes cartel members killed the snitch's family as punishment for ratting them out. Which was why getting anyone to testify against them was difficult.

He turned toward Golden. "I need to get Ms. Hall out

of here and somewhere safe. I've contacted my boss, Captain Rhy Finnegan, to let him know about the shooting. He may want to work with your captain about getting results from the evidence collection." He snapped his fingers. "I almost forgot. I returned fire and struck the truck. I don't think the bullet did much damage, though, because they sped out of here without stopping."

"We can be on the lookout for a black truck sporting a bullet hole," Avery said.

He nodded, even though he suspected the shooters would have ditched the truck by now and picked up something else.

At least, that's what he would have done.

"We may need to get the local DEA involved too," Golden said with a frown. "If the cartel is here, they'll want to know."

"Yeah, okay." He should have thought of that for himself. Roscoe doubted the DEA knew anything about the break-in back in Texas, though. "You can let the DEA here know that I worked with an agent by the name of Charlie Olson down south. They should collaborate on this." In his humble opinion, the more law enforcement officers involved, the better. "I'd be happy to talk to the DEA agent here in Milwaukee once I have Ms. Hall safe."

"Good idea." Golden took a step back and lifted his hand to his radio.

Roscoe turned toward Libby. She looked pale and exhausted. Traumatized by finding her place broken into, threatened with a knife, then being followed and shot at. Not to mention traveling across the country. "Can you give me a few more minutes to grab some gear? Then we'll hit the road."

She nodded and sank back down onto the edge of the

sofa. He hurried to the guest bedroom and tossed some things in a duffel bag. Then he called Cameron, who was out of town for the week visiting his girlfriend in Madison. His cousin didn't answer, so he left a message instructing him to stay away from the house until they talked.

Hoping Cameron would call him back sooner rather than later, he joined Libby in the living room. Officer Golden crossed toward him. "I need your contact information. And Ms. Hall's too. I've been told that a DEA agent by the name of Doug Bridges wants to chat with both of you."

"Fine." He quickly rattled off his cell phone. "There's no point in taking down Ms. Hall's number; we're not keeping that phone."

"Oh, yeah. That makes sense." Golden frowned. "How will Bridges get in touch with her?"

"Through me." He caught Libby's startled gaze. "I'm sorry, Libby, but we don't know how these guys tracked you. We can't risk keeping that phone."

"I understand." She dug in her purse, then held it out to him. "Take it. I don't want those men to find me again."

He took it, powered it down, then stomped on it with his foot, grinding his heel into the device until it was destroyed. Then he picked up the pieces and tossed them into the garbage. Returning to Libby's side, he held out his hand to help her up. "Let's go."

"I have a suitcase in my car," Libby said.

He hesitated, then nodded, realizing she needed proper maternity clothes. The fact that she was pregnant with their child was still a shocker. Yet he couldn't allow her condition to sidetrack him. There would be time to discuss that more later.

Once they were safe.

He slung the duffel over his shoulder and grabbed the

keys to the squad. The good news was that his truck was at the precinct where there was no way the gunmen could have seen it. Once they'd spoken to Bridges, they could head out in his vehicle.

"Stay behind me," he said in a low voice. "We'll get your suitcase, then climb into the squad."

She nodded without saying anything. Her wide eyes spoke volumes as he pushed open the front door and stepped out onto the porch. He scanned the surrounding neighborhood but didn't see anything alarming.

As promised, Libby hung back, allowing him to lead the way. When he stopped at the trunk of her car, she bumped into him.

"Sorry." She sounded embarrassed. Then she clicked the key fob to open the trunk. Her suitcase was small and looked brand new. It gave him pause.

He glanced at her over his shoulder. "Did you buy this along the way?"

"Yes. I drove without stopping until Oklahoma, then stopped in Illinois to buy the suitcase, prenatal vitamins, and a change of clothes. Why?"

"Cash or credit?" Even as he asked, he knew.

"Credit. I don't carry that much cash around." Realization dawned. "They tracked my credit card?"

"Possibly." Although he wondered why they hadn't picked her up at one of the gas stations along the way. Maybe she had already been halfway through Illinois by the time they had gotten a hold of her credit card information.

He lifted her pink suitcase out of the back and carried it to the squad. He set it down to open the passenger door for her. Moments later, he was backing down the driveway, keeping a wary eye out for the black truck.

There was a long silence before she spoke. "I guess you're wondering about the baby."

"Yeah, although I'm mostly wondering why you didn't reach out to me as soon as you found out the news." He cast a sidelong glance at her. "I would have come back to Texas."

She grimaced. "I didn't want you to be a part of my baby's life."

That casual comment was like a donkey kick to the chest. "What do you mean? I'm the baby's father, aren't I?"

"Yes. But you only pretended to care about me to get to my brother." She averted her gaze, staring out the window. "You really hurt me, Roscoe."

"I'm sorry." He tried to think of a way to reassure her. "I wasn't dating you only to get to your brother. I cared about you, Libby."

"Yeah, sure." She shook her head, and his stomach twisted when he saw the glint of tears in her eyes. "I don't believe you. Just drop it, okay? That doesn't matter now. It's your fault I'm in danger in the first place."

His fault? He grimaced, following her logic. "Because I arrested Tony."

"Yes." She sighed. "I understand you had a job to do and that my brother was mixed up in a dangerous crowd. I know that. But somehow I'm the one with a target on my back."

That was all true. But if anyone else had arrested Tony, she would be in the same situation.

His gaze dropped to her belly, then darted back to the road. *Almost the same situation,* he silently amended. Maybe if he hadn't arrested Tony, he and Libby would still be together.

"I'm sorry you're in this predicament. If I had known you would be in danger, I wouldn't have left. I was under the impression that Tony would be moved to a prison out of state and the cartel would never know who had given them up."

She shrugged but still didn't meet his gaze. "Whatever."

Maybe she had a reason to be angry with him. He had gotten to know her because she was Tony's sister. But his feelings for her had been real. He'd been attracted to her the first time he saw her, checking groceries at the store, a part-time job she held during the summers and on weekends. He would have dated her no matter what his job entailed.

Yet he also knew their night together shouldn't have happened. She'd been reeling from hearing about her father's heart attack, and he'd allowed things to go too far.

A week later, he'd arrested Tony. When she learned he was a cop, she'd told him to get lost and never come back. He'd foolishly taken her at her word. His boss had told him that he should get out of the state for a while until everything had settled down with the drug cartel. He'd heard about the opening on the tactical team from his cousin, Cam, and had applied, never expecting to get the job.

Thankfully, Rhy had hired him, and he was just starting to feel like a member of the team, rather than the outsider.

Yet he knew he'd give up his role on the team and more to support Libby and their child.

He pulled his wayward thoughts together with an effort. This wasn't the time to dream about what his future might look like. They needed to find the gunmen and uncover who had sent them chasing her over several state lines.

The more he thought about Libby being followed all the way from Texas, the more he realized this never should have happened.

Was there a leak inside the prison system? One of the guards or maybe an inside informant?

Or was the leak within law enforcement, either the border patrol or the DEA?

He was about to call Rhy to let him know his concerns when he saw a large black truck coming up fast on his tail.

"Hang on," he warned, punching the gas and cranking the wheel.

"Roscoe!" Libby grabbed the handrest, clinging onto it for dear life. "Is the truck back?"

He took a sharp right-hand turn, then hit the gas again to put more distance between them. He flipped on the overhead lights and sirens to force everyone around him to get out of the way.

A crack of gunfire followed by the shattering of the back window of the squad only made things worse. He had a clear path ahead of him but so did the truck.

He managed to key his radio. "Unit fourteen requesting backup! Taking gunfire from a black Chevy truck!"

"Roger that, unit fourteen. What's your twenty?"

He didn't have time to respond when another crack of gunfire echoed from behind him. Roscoe wrenched the wheel to the left and headed toward the precinct.

Praying they'd get there before another round disabled the squad, leaving them as sitting ducks with nowhere to hide.

CHAPTER TWO

The black truck had found them!

Libby huddled in the front seat of the squad, bending over as far as her six-months-pregnant belly would allow. She feared it wouldn't be good enough, that at any moment a bullet would make it through the car to find its mark.

Please, Lord, keep us safe!

She gripped the arm rest tightly as Roscoe made one quick turn after another as traffic parted for them like the Red Sea. It would have been impressive if not for the black truck keeping pace behind them. Or so she assumed, as she didn't lift her head to see for herself.

"Officer needs assistance," Roscoe barked. She noticed he'd lost some of his Texas twang in the months he'd been gone.

More sirens joined the one wailing from their squad. Hope filled her heart as she continued to silently pray for safety. Especially for her baby.

"The black truck has turned west on Forest Hills Avenue," Roscoe said. "I need an officer to take up the chase!"

"Roger that," the calm dispatch voice said. There was no way Libby could ever be that cool and collected in a situation like this.

Then again, the dispatcher wasn't being fired upon.

She gingerly lifted her head. "The shooters are gone?"

"Yeah." Roscoe thumped his fist on the steering wheel. "I hope the officers back there can find the truck. I hate the idea of them getting away."

She silently agreed. Placing a hand on her belly, she took several deep breaths to calm her racing heart. "How did they find us?"

"Not sure." Roscoe sent her a quick glance. "Could be they parked somewhere nearby and waited for us to leave. The squad was sitting in the driveway, which made it easy to spot."

"But how did they know which way we would go?" It was difficult to comprehend.

"Maybe they had a pair of binoculars and a direct line of sight." He scowled and slowed his speed to a less reckless pace. He silenced the siren, a blessing to her ears, but kept the red and blue lights flashing. "I should have sent officers out to canvass the area right away."

"This isn't your fault," she protested. If she were honest, she'd admit he wasn't really to blame for the situation at all. Tony had been the one involved with the cartel. As a teacher, she hated the idea of kids being exposed to drugs.

"I'm starting to think it is," he said grimly.

She wanted to ask more, but he turned into the parking lot of a police station. She glanced around curiously as several officers came out of the building toward them. She pushed out of the vehicle, and Roscoe grabbed the duffel bag, then came over to stand beside her.

"Anyone hurt?" a tall blond-haired man asked.

"No." Roscoe glanced at her.

"I'm okay." Being scared to death probably didn't count.

"We're fine, Rhy," Roscoe said. "But you'll want to get the crime scene techs out here. There's a slug in the back of my driver's seat."

"What?" She gasped in horror. "How do you know?"

"I felt the impact." Roscoe shrugged. "Thankfully, there's a metal plate back there that prevented the bullet from getting all the way through."

Her knees became weak as she realized just how close Roscoe had come to dying. Maybe she was still angry with him for how he'd used her to get to her brother, but she didn't want him dead.

"Hey, are you okay?" Roscoe's voice held concern. "You look like you're going to pass out."

"It's just a lot to deal with." Her voice sounded shaky, so she tried again. "I'm scared, but I won't faint."

"Maybe you should sit down," a tall, dark-haired man said kindly. "Especially in your condition."

"Joe's right. Let's get you inside." Roscoe cupped his hand around her elbow to usher her toward the front door. "There's bottled water in the kitchenette."

Going along with him was easier than arguing. Besides, drinking some water sounded good.

"I need to know when the black truck has been found," Roscoe said as he opened the door for her.

"We'll hear as soon as they have it," Joe assured him. "Rhy had already let the local police know we want to be involved."

"I'm sure they won't be happy about that," Roscoe muttered.

"Oh, I think they'll accept the support." Rhy shrugged. "Besides, anyone who shoots at a cop gets top priority from all officers in the entire area, regardless of jurisdiction."

One could argue a pregnant woman being targeted should get the same consideration, but she managed to hold her tongue. All that mattered was that the gunmen were found and arrested.

And if the fact that a cop was targeted inspired the rest of the law enforcement community to band together, so be it.

"Have a seat." Roscoe led her to an empty desk. He set the duffel on the floor at her feet. "I need to grab the suitcase, then I'll get you that water."

She sank into the chair, glancing around curiously. This was where Roscoe worked. It was interesting that he'd made his home here in Milwaukee, about as far from Rio Grande City as possible.

A few minutes passed before Roscoe returned with her pink suitcase and a bottle of water. "Here you go."

"Thanks." She took a grateful sip.

"Is the safe house available?" Roscoe had directed the question to Rhy.

"Unfortunately not." Rhy grimaced. "Let's call around and see if we can find a hotel for you. I'm thinking the City Central Hotel or the Timberland Falls Suites may not be fully booked for the holiday."

"Okay, that's fine." Roscoe looked disappointed at the news. "But I'd like Libby to be put on the list for the safe house as soon as it's open."

"I can do that," Rhy agreed. "Libby, I'm Captain Rhy Finnegan, and this is Lieutenant Joe Kingsley. We want you to know that your safety is our top priority."

"Thank you." She managed a smile. "It's nice to meet you both."

"Likewise, although it would be better if you weren't in danger." Joe turned toward Roscoe. "You think this is related to a Mexican drug cartel?"

"Yeah, I do." Roscoe hesitated, glanced at her, then continued. "Libby Hall's older brother, Tony, was involved with drug trafficking. I was able to arrest him with the help of the DEA and border patrol. It sounds as if Tony has agreed to testify against the cartel. However, Libby's apartment was ransacked, a large knife stuck in the kitchen table as a threat, possibly in retaliation to Tony's cooperation with the feds. She was scared enough to come all the way here, only to have picked up a tail at the Wisconsin and Illinois border. The black truck showed up at my place, then again after we left to come here."

"Don't like the sound of that," Joe said darkly. "Why not just kill Tony? Why go after his family?"

"Typical behavior for the cartel," Roscoe said. "They want people to suffer, and what better way to do that than to threaten and kill their loved ones."

Hearing him summarize her life in the past few days made her feel sick. First losing her dad, then Roscoe's betrayal. She didn't have any other family aside from Tony. Her mother had died when she was only ten. Their housekeeper, Nancy, had been like a mother to her, and Libby had been just as upset when Nancy had passed away two years ago too. Her dad . . . she hadn't been close to him as his job kept him busy.

A wave of nausea had her putting a hand to her stomach, willing it to settle down.

"Do you need to eat something?" Rhy asked.

"Maybe," she admitted. She didn't have any sort of appetite, but her body was clearly telling her something was amiss.

"You look the way my wife does when she misses a meal," Rhy said. "Pregnancy means eating, even when you don't feel like it."

"True that. My wife, Elly, is pregnant. She can be throwing up one minute and eating the next." Joe grinned, clearly thrilled with his wife's condition.

"We'll stop on the way to the hotel," Roscoe said. "I just need a few minutes to make sure we can get a room."

"I'm okay," she lied.

"I'll make the calls," Rhy offered. "Stay here with Libby."

"Actually, I'd like to get a vest for her," Roscoe said. "I know it won't protect the baby as much as I'd like, but it's better than nothing."

"Fine with me." Rhy turned away. "I'll be back in a minute."

Roscoe went to find a vest, leaving her with the dark-haired Joe. She was a little surprised by how they'd rallied around her and Roscoe. Apparently, they took this whole idea of teamwork to heart.

"Hey, Roscoe is a good cop. He'll keep you safe." Joe smiled encouragingly. "I would trust him with my life and that of my wife and unborn child."

"I know he will." Roscoe hadn't seemed upset about the baby. Shocked, confused, dazed, but not angry.

Knowing his baby's life was at risk would no doubt be enough for him to protect her at all costs.

It was only after she delivered their baby that she had to worry about what the future would bring. Somehow, she did not see Roscoe giving up any rights to his child.

A fact that would make her life extremely difficult.

ROSCOE STOOD for a moment in the equipment room, searching for the strength to remain calm. Now that they were safe in the precinct, reality had settled in with a vengeance.

The shooter had gotten far too close.

And he couldn't help but think Libby was right to blame him. He had used his attraction to her to get information on her brother, Tony. When he'd found the drugs in Tony's apartment, he'd participated in a sting operation with Charlie Olson and the border patrol agents to pull Tony's semitruck over. They found drugs hidden behind the door panels and inside the seat cushions and arrested Tony on the spot. When Libby found out, she'd tossed him out of her life. Obviously before she realized she was pregnant.

Now her house had been broken into, and the shooter had traveled across numerous state lines to eliminate Libby and their baby.

Yeah. This was definitely his fault.

He searched for a vest that he thought would fit the best. It wouldn't be enough. He'd be happier placing her in the safe house lined with bulletproof glass, but that wasn't an option.

He carried the vest over to her. "Let's try this on for size."

She gave it a dubious look, then rose to her feet. The vest had Velcro straps, and the lower set just managed to cover her abdomen.

"It's not perfect, but it will have to do." He met her gaze. "It will be heavy and hot in the July sun."

"That's fine." She shrugged, glancing down at the vest, then back up at him. "The summer weather is much nicer here than back home."

"Yeah, it is." The winters were brutal, but he decided against bringing that up now. Once the danger was over, they'd have to discuss how they'd raise this child together.

"Roscoe?" Rhy strode purposefully toward them. "I got you a suite at the City Central Hotel."

"Great." He gave his boss a nod. "Appreciate the help."

"Of course. Oh, and the black truck was found abandoned about ten blocks from where the shootout occurred." Rhy scowled and shrugged. "The crime scene techs are sweeping the truck for DNA and fingerprints. I'm sure they'll find something useful. Most likely sweat as that's harder to eliminate than simply wearing gloves."

"I hope you're right." Obtaining the shooter's DNA was a great lead. The only downside was that DNA took time to process.

Time they may not have.

"No sign of the shooters?" Libby asked.

"No, but there are teams of officers canvassing the area," Rhy explained. "Hopefully, they'll find witnesses who can offer some assistance in describing these guys."

"What about traffic cameras?" Roscoe asked. "Can you ask Gabe to take a look at those too?"

"Already on it." Rhy waved a hand. "We have the investigation under control. Why don't you get Libby something to eat and get situated at the hotel? We'll keep you updated as we learn anything new."

"Okay. But there's one more thing. Officer Golden mentioned getting the DEA involved, some guy by the name of Doug Bridges." Roscoe eyed Rhy somberly. "Are you sure we can trust him?"

"Yes, absolutely. Bridges is a good cop. My brother Brady and our cousin Marc Callahan have worked with him on several cases in the past." Rhy nodded thoughtfully.

"That's a great idea to get Doug involved. I'll have him follow up with you, okay?"

"Yeah, the sooner the better." He turned to Libby. He slung the duffel over his shoulder, then picked up the suitcase. "Ready to go? My truck is out back."

"Sure." She looked better, not as pale and shaky. It wasn't right that she had to dodge gunmen and bullets while being pregnant.

Two attempts on her life in the past few hours were unthinkable. Yet the more he thought about his role in arresting Tony Hall, the more he realized that he was just as much of a target as Libby.

Maybe more so. That bullet that had embedded in the back of his driver's side seat had absolutely been intended for him.

There had to be a leak somewhere within the Texas law enforcement community. A leak he hoped this Doug Bridges could help identify and eliminate. He was glad Bridges was with the DEA.

Yet if the leak was elsewhere, like in the prison itself, then Bridges might not have the leverage needed to ferret it out.

Should he stash Libby somewhere and head down to Texas? He didn't like the idea of leaving her, yet he had a bad feeling that staying in Milwaukee wouldn't be smart. The original drug trafficking had taken place in Rio Grande City. Yet the shooting had taken place here.

As he opened the truck door for her, she said, "You drive a black truck too?"

"What can I say? Black is better for hiding at night." After storing their items in the back, he offered her a hand, watching with a hint of amusement as she struggled to get up into the passenger seat. Then he sobered, realizing that her condition would make a quick getaway more difficult.

Hopefully, it wouldn't matter. Once they were situated in the hotel, she would be safe.

Although being with the tactical team over the past six months had shown him that safety was often an illusion. Several of his teammates had been in dicey situations recently, barely escaping with their lives. Most recently Grayson's now fiancée, Dr. Eve Shaw, had been the target of a conspiracy to kill her.

The enormity of the responsibility of keeping Libby and their baby safe weighed on his shoulders. But he did his best not to let it crush him. "What would you like to eat?"

"Anything with protein."

He glanced at her. "Baby likes protein?"

"Yep. Maybe a chicken sandwich?"

"Sure, I know a great place." He glanced at his watch, realizing it was midafternoon. No wonder she was hungry. "We'll use the drive-through, then head to the hotel. It's not far."

"Sounds good." She tugged at the vest. "You weren't kidding about this being heavy and hot."

"Yeah, well, it's only for a little while longer." He cranked the air-conditioning, knowing that once they were in the hotel, she could take the vest off.

The drive-through restaurant didn't take long, and soon they had their respective crispy chicken sandwiches in hand.

"Dear Lord Jesus, thank You for this food we are about to eat. We ask You to keep us all safe in Your care. Amen," Libby said.

"Amen," he answered. "When did you start attending church?"

"After you left." She glanced at her stomach. "The women were surprisingly supportive."

"I'm glad." He'd gotten used to praying before meals since most of his teammates were believers. His foster parents had been too. But he'd drifted from the church prior to joining the team.

She glanced at him in surprise, then unwrapped her sandwich. He set his aside, preferring to keep both hands on the wheel and his attention on the road.

The shooters had abandoned the black truck, but it was possible they had found another vehicle to use. Not that they should be able to track his personal vehicle.

Still, he wasn't taking any chances. If there was a leak within law enforcement, things like license plate numbers and other identifying information could be found relatively easily.

Maybe he'd ask Rhy to provide a clean ride once they were at the hotel. He wouldn't feel safe until he had Libby off the street.

"It's so different here," she said between bites. "Way more buildings and traffic."

"Yeah, it's a much bigger city than what we're used to." He'd had to spend time studying local maps so he wouldn't get lost. "It's been a cultural change as well."

"You like it here?" The question was casual, but a quick glance at Libby proved it was anything but.

"I like the job and the teamwork of being in the tactical unit. Having four seasons is nice too." He shrugged. "But I still miss home." Not that he had a home to go back to.

Except, maybe he did. It suddenly occurred to him that anywhere his child was located would be home.

She nodded thoughtfully but didn't say anything more.

He figured this was a prelude to the *what-are-we-going-to-do-once-the-baby-is-born* conversation.

Too bad he had no idea how they would make things work.

She had finished her meal by the time they reached the City Central Hotel. He pulled into the parking lot, grabbed his sandwich, and slid out from behind the wheel. "I'll escort you inside, then bring in the luggage."

"Thanks." She awkwardly climbed out of the truck. They definitely needed a replacement vehicle, one that would be easier for her to get in and out of.

As they headed inside, the desk clerk eyed Libby's vest warily. "May I help you?"

"Roscoe Turner, we have a suite."

"Ah, yes. Of course." She took a moment to pull up the paperwork and the two room keys. "Sign here. Your room is down the hall on the left."

"I know, thanks." He pushed the paperwork back and handed Libby one of the keys. The suite was one the team had used before.

Libby looked around, her eyes wide. "This is nice."

"Make yourself comfortable. I'll grab the luggage." He headed back outside, then took a moment to pull the truck around to the side entrance. After bringing their respective bags in, he glanced at her. "Which bedroom do you want? I'll set your suitcase inside."

"That one is fine." She gestured to the bedroom on the right.

After putting her pink suitcase on the bed, he carried his duffel to the other room. They were about the same size, and each had its own bathroom. He was glad Rhy had suggested the place for Libby's sake.

He returned to the main living area. "I hope you don't mind if I eat."

"Of course not." She sat beside him, playing with her water bottle. His chicken sandwich was no longer warm, but he quickly devoured it anyway. "I should tell you that I have not spoken to the Rio Grande City police about the break-in. My apartment door was broken, and the knife was an obvious threat, so I'm sure they're looking for me."

He arched a brow. "Actually, I'm glad to hear that. I think I'd rather have that information go through Rhy, Joe, or maybe even a lawyer to add a layer of protection between you and the authorities."

She frowned. "You really don't trust them?"

"Nope." There was no hesitation in his tone. "From this point forward, we don't trust anyone except my teammates and this Doug Bridges guy."

She ripped at the label on the water bottle. "I still can't believe this is happening. That I'm in danger."

"I know. I wish things were different, but we will get through this." He longed to draw her into his arms but managed to hold back. His feelings for her were real, but when she'd lashed out at him for arresting Tony, he'd accepted there was no chance of a future.

But that was before he'd known she was pregnant with his child. Now they had a future together, whether she liked it or not.

"I don't understand why they broke into my apartment," she said with a troubled frown. "Why they'd stuck a knife in the middle of my kitchen table."

"The knife was a warning, so I'm really glad you got out of there." He hated to think about what might have happened if she had been home when the cartel had shown up. "I wish you would have called to tell me about the baby.

I would have dropped everything to return to Texas. I would never abandon you like that."

She scoffed. "Yeah, well, you said a lot of things, Roscoe. Most of them weren't true."

He supposed he deserved that. He started to say something, but his phone rang. He hesitated upon seeing the unknown number on the screen. It was local, though, so he pressed the talk button. "Yeah?"

"Officer Roscoe Turner? This is Doug Bridges with the DEA. I hear you've been tangling with the cartel."

He relaxed. "Yeah, you could say that."

"I'm five minutes from the City Central Hotel. Don't be surprised by a knock at the door, okay? Rhy gave me your room number."

"Understood. See you soon." He ended the call. "Bridges will be here any minute. He's going to want to hear the entire story."

"I know." She shrugged. "Although I'm not sure how a DEA agent from Milwaukee can help us."

"He'll have connections within the agency, but I understand your concern." He considered mentioning the idea of going back to Rio Grande City but decided to wait to see how this meeting with Bridges went. The guy must know a fair amount about the drug trade in general. And since lots of drugs were coming in from the southern border, with the northern border a close second, there could be cartel members working in this area too.

Hearing a knock at the door, he rose. He used the peephole, smiling when he saw the badge Bridges held up.

"Come in," he said, stepping back to make room. "I'm Roscoe Turner, and this is Libby Hall."

"You're Tony Hall's sister, correct?" Bridges said as he joined her at the table.

"Yes. But I don't want you to think I condone his drug trafficking, because I don't." Her green eyes flashed. "I had no idea Tony had gotten himself involved with the cartel. It was a stupid thing for him to do."

"Yeah. Well, about that." Bridges cleared his throat, glanced at Roscoe, then turned back to Libby. "I'm sorry to tell you this, but your brother was found dead in his cell. Ironically, it looks to be from a drug overdose."

"What? How is that possible?" Libby asked shakily. "How could drugs be sneaked into the prison?"

"There's an investigation underway, but I thought you should know." Bridges turned to Roscoe. "Your revenge theory is playing out big time."

Roscoe nodded numbly.

There wasn't a doubt in his mind that he and Libby were next on the cartel's hit list.

CHAPTER THREE

Tony was dead. Murdered, even while he was incarcerated. Grief hit hard, even though she and Tony hadn't been especially close. The four-year age gap between them was such that he had ignored her while they were younger, treating her as if she was a nuisance. And obviously, Tony had made several bad choices along the way, especially getting involved in the cartel.

But he hadn't deserved to die.

Her chest felt heavy. Losing her mother at a young age, now her father and her brother was devastating. She was an orphan.

A woman without a family.

The baby in her womb kicked, reminding her she did have a family. Yet a woman on the run didn't have much to offer a child.

"Libby? Are you okay?" Roscoe's voice interrupted her troubled thoughts.

"It's not right." Her voice was hoarse. "Tony should have been safe in prison."

Doug Bridges and Roscoe exchanged a long glance.

"Unfortunately, a lot of bad things can happen in prison." Doug's expression was serious. "But you are right that murder shouldn't be one of them."

She placed her hand on her abdomen, doing her best to soothe the baby. And herself. "You believe the cartel will keep coming after me? Even if Tony is no longer a threat?"

"Yes, I'm afraid so." Doug reached over to rest his hand on her knee. "I'm sorry, Libby, but I need to know everything about the cartel your brother was involved with."

A flash of anger hit hard. She almost smacked his hand away. "I don't know anything! Ask Roscoe! He dated me just to get information on Tony. Whatever he learned was enough to arrest my brother. I was clueless."

Doug nodded, then turned toward Roscoe. "Tell me what you know."

Roscoe glanced at her as if he didn't want to tell the story while she sat there listening. Well, too bad. She wasn't going anywhere. Not if these drug runners sought to do her harm.

"I was asked by DEA Agent Charlie Olson to help them on a case. They had gotten a glimpse of Tony near one of the drug drops and wanted more intel on him. I was asked to get close to the Hall family to see what I could uncover." Roscoe rose and began to pace the room. "Tony was a loner, seemed to keep to himself. I couldn't find any close friends to talk to. It seemed like people knew of Tony but didn't know him well enough to talk to him."

"That's where I came in," Libby said with a bite to her tone. "You figured I would be the easiest way to get to my brother."

He stared at her for a moment, then nodded slowly. "I can't deny that is the reason I sought you out, Libby. I learned you were a middle school teacher and that you also worked part time on the weekends at the grocery store."

She averted her gaze, remembering how handsome she'd thought Roscoe when he came to the grocery store every Saturday, seemingly always waiting in her line. When he asked her out for a coffee, she'd been thrilled.

It had never occurred to her that he only wanted information about her brother.

"Tony was a truck driver, spending his time on the road." Roscoe went on. "He was crossing the border on a regular basis, allegedly that was one of his usual routes. Only as it turned out, he was moving drugs for the cartel."

A sudden chill snaked down her spine. Her father had been a truck driver too. Until he had been diagnosed with heart disease. He'd had an episode where he'd blacked out, which had ended his career, putting him on disability. In truth, she hadn't been totally shocked at her father's heart attack. He had not bothered to live a healthy lifestyle.

But drugs? No, she wasn't going there. Just because her father and Tony had crossed the US-Mexico border for their job didn't mean her father had ever been involved in drug trafficking.

That had been Tony's bad decision. Not her father's.

"How did you find the evidence needed to arrest Tony?" Doug asked.

She closed her eyes for a moment, knowing that she was responsible for that outcome. "I happened to mention I had a key to Tony's apartment. My brother often asked me to get his mail and take care of the garbage while he was on the road." She glanced at Roscoe. "I was foolish enough to take Roscoe with me."

"I found several boxes in the closet," Roscoe said, taking

up the story. "I managed to get a look inside and saw packages of fentanyl. I took pictures and showed them to Charlie." He shrugged, avoiding her gaze. "From there, I worked with the DEA to track Tony's route. I was there when they pulled him over. He denied having drugs, and I have to admit they were hidden extremely well. But we found them tucked into the truck's interior door frames and arrested him on the spot."

There was a long moment of silence. She supposed she should give Roscoe credit for coming to tell her about her brother's arrest. And the role he'd played in it.

"Did Tony give you any indication who hired him?" Doug asked.

"No, he lawyered up." Roscoe shrugged. "Then his lawyer reached out, claiming he wanted to make a deal for a lesser sentence."

"Okay, so from that point on, the DEA took over the case?" Doug pressed. "The local police were no longer involved?"

"Correct." Roscoe glanced at her. "I was actually a cop in San Antonio but was asked to do this undercover stint in Rio Grande City."

No wonder she hadn't recognized him. Not that she knew the local cops by name. Still, she saw a lot of familiar faces working in the grocery store each week.

It suddenly occurred to her that she didn't know anything about the real Roscoe Turner. Not even that he'd lived in San Antonio. Did he have other family aside from Cameron? How much of what he'd told her was real?

And how much was a big fat lie?

WITH EVERY WORD ROSCOE SPOKE, he could see Libby retreating into her shell, distancing herself from him. And there was nothing he could do to change it.

At least, not yet.

He wanted to believe she would eventually forgive him. That she would come to understand his only goal had been to get a drug trafficker off the streets.

Maybe he should have told her about how his own birth mother had died of a drug overdose when he was barely two years old. That he'd been in the car with her while she'd overdosed.

And that he'd been placed in foster care, then ultimately adopted by the Turners.

"I plan to reach out to Charlie Olson," Bridges said, interrupting his thoughts. "I would like to know what intel, if any, they got out of Tony prior to his death."

"You mean his murder," Libby said sharply. "Tony may have been taking drugs across the border, but he'd never touched them himself. He wasn't like that."

"I know your brother was clean," Roscoe said with a nod. "I suspect he was sucked in by the lure of easy money."

She scowled. "Did you ever think that maybe Tony didn't have a choice? That maybe he'd been told he needed to cooperate with the cartel or be killed?"

He was taken aback by her suggestion. "Is that what Tony told you?"

"He wouldn't tell me anything," she admitted. "I visited him in prison, but he wouldn't say much." She stared down at her lap for a moment, then added, "He saw I was pregnant and told me to get out of the city and move somewhere else."

"Wait a minute, how long ago did you visit him?" Roscoe asked.

"Two weeks ago." Realization dawned on her features. "You think that's why the cartel broke into my apartment?"

"The timing is suspicious." He blew out a breath, then turned to Bridges. "I believe there's a leak in the prison or within the law enforcement community. Libby visits her brother, then two weeks later she experiences a break-in with a knife stuck in her kitchen table. Maybe the cartel thinks he told her something important."

"Maybe they did, but I have to say, issuing a mere warning isn't their style," Bridges mused. "The cartel is vicious when it comes to protecting their product and their network. If they thought she knew something that could implicate them, they would have waited in the apartment and killed her."

Libby sucked in a quick breath, placing her hand over her mouth in horror. As much as he wished Bridges hadn't been so blunt, there was no doubt the DEA agent was speaking the truth.

"I don't understand it either," Roscoe admitted. "But it's clear that regardless of the initial warning, they're playing for keeps now."

"Yeah, I get that." Bridges thought for a moment, then said, "Do you trust Charlie Olson?"

"I don't trust anyone but you and the tactical team," he said without hesitation. "Everyone else is a suspect until proven otherwise."

"I hear you, and I'll tread carefully," Bridges agreed. "I won't reveal your location or Libby's either. But I need something to go on. If the DEA doesn't have any suspects, we're not going to get very far on this."

Doug was right. "I know. There's the abandoned black Chevy truck, but it's going to take time to process the evidence. We have the two slugs taken from the house, but that won't help unless we get a ballistics match in the system." He abruptly straightened. "Although if the shooters are members of the cartel, there is a chance their weapons have been used in other crimes."

"I'll jump on that; getting a match would be great." Bridges glanced between the two of them. "Anything else either of you can think of? No other known friends of Tony Hall?"

"My brother didn't have many friends," Libby said. "He claimed he was on the road too much to get close to people. But I think he preferred to be alone."

"I didn't find any friends when I was gathering intel," Roscoe said. "I mean, some people claimed they knew him, had gone to school with him or whatever. But not a single person seemed to know anything about his recent activities."

"That's not very helpful." Doug sighed then rose to his feet. "I'll make calls and bug the techs about processing evidence. In the meantime, you two need to stay off the grid."

"That's why we're here," Roscoe agreed. He stood to walk Bridges to the door. "Thanks for your help."

"Anytime." Bridges scowled. "I don't like the way drugs are flowing into the country like water. It seems the moment we shut off one spigot, another springs forth. The flow is relentless, but every truck load or trafficker we take off the streets is a step forward. Even though I hate knowing it's a very small step."

"Yeah." Roscoe could see that Doug Bridges was dedicated to his job, but that he was also frustrated by the lack of progress. Something he could relate to. "Stay in touch. I'd like to know if you come up with a list of suspects."

"Will do. Later." Bridges shook his hand and left. Roscoe made sure to close and lock the door behind him. He turned to see Libby sitting with her head back on the sofa cushion, her eyes closed.

She looked fragile and strong at the same time. How was it possible that being pregnant made her more attractive? He'd thought she was pretty when they'd first met, but now she glowed. Or maybe it was just not seeing her for the past six months that made him so hyperaware of her.

Her quick thinking in leaving her apartment, without taking anything with her, had likely saved her life.

If she hadn't? He didn't like to think about the possibility of learning about Libby's pregnancy only after she and the baby were dead.

Stepping softly, he moved toward the kitchenette. He considered making a pot of coffee but didn't want to wake her.

"I wish this was over," Libby said in a tired voice. Opening her eyes, she stared at him. "I can't help but think I'll spend the rest of my life running from the cartel."

"You won't." He injected confidence into his tone. "We're going to get to the bottom of this. Try not to worry. I'm sure stress isn't good for you and the baby."

"Easier said than done." She sighed. "I keep seeing that knife sticking out of my kitchen table. And hearing the crack of gunfire. It's hard to imagine someone would ruthlessly kill a pregnant woman."

He wished he could take all of that away from her, but that was impossible. As Doug had said, the cartel was known to be brutal and violent. Worse, they didn't have much of anything to go on. Then he had an idea. "I have my laptop in my duffel bag. What do you think about going through some mug shots to see if anyone looks familiar to you?"

"Why would they?" Her green eyes glinted with anger. "I told you I didn't even know Tony was bringing drugs across the border. I wasn't even that close to my brother. He never introduced me to anyone he worked with."

"I know but hear me out." He crossed over to sit beside her on the sofa. "You worked in the grocery store every weekend. Even drug traffickers have to eat. It's possible you'll recognize someone that we can link to your brother."

Her gaze was doubtful. "You really think so? Or are you just doing this to keep me busy?"

"I really think so." The more he thought about it, the more he liked the idea. "You may even recognize someone who had been hanging out around your brother's apartment. Maybe a neighbor or something."

"I doubt that." She didn't look convinced. Then she shrugged. "Fine, if you want me to try, I will. But don't get your hopes up that anything will come of this. I didn't make it a habit to memorize strangers' faces."

"Thanks, Libby." He rose. "Do you mind if I make a pot of coffee?"

"Help yourself." She grimaced. "I have to admit coffee is the one thing I miss the most."

"Would you rather I didn't make it?" He would give coffee up, too, if that helped her cope. It wouldn't be easy, but he'd do it.

"Don't be silly. You should enjoy it." She rubbed her hands over the part of her stomach that wasn't covered by the bullet-resistant vest. "Can I take this off while we're inside the suite? Sitting is not comfortable while wearing it."

"Sure." He leaned over to help undo the Velcro straps.

After setting the vest aside, he headed into his room to grab his computer and set it up on the table.

Then he proceeded to make coffee. "I should have asked Doug to bring some lemonade with him. I know that's your favorite."

She came over to sit at the table. "I'm surprised you remember."

He remembered everything about their time together. "We can order lemonade and snacks from room service in a bit."

"That's fine." She gestured to the computer. "Do you have access to a criminal database?"

"I do." He turned the computer toward him so he could use the hotel's internet to connect to the police database. He set up a search using Mexican cartels as one of the criteria, along with the location of south Texas. The computer icon whirled for a while, no doubt the database was huge, before the first few pictures bloomed on the screen. "Here you go." He turned the computer toward her. "Take your time. We're safe here, so there's no reason to rush."

She nodded, then leaned forward to begin going through photos. He waited for the coffee to finish brewing, then joined her at the table. He stationed himself partially behind her so he could see the pictures over her shoulder. Some she passed by quickly, especially those who sported a lot of facial or neck tattoos. Others she looked at for a long few seconds before moving onto the next.

This was a long shot, but he thought Libby appreciated having something to do to help pass the time. He also thought Libby was more in tune to her surroundings than she was giving herself credit for.

She had once confessed to him that she'd noticed a

sketchy-looking guy hanging around the middle school during the afternoon recess period. She'd gone as far as to call the local police who ended up arresting him. Turned out the guy was a sexual predator who was ordered by the court to stay far away from schools and other places where kids were gathered.

Thanks to Libby's keen eye, the scumbag was back in jail where he belonged.

The next two hours passed slowly. A few times Libby stopped to rub her eyes, but then continued going through the mug shots. He rose and paced the length of the room, feeling restless.

His phone rang. Seeing Doug Bridges's name on the screen, he quickly answered. "Did you find something?"

"The slugs that were taken out of your cousin's house match the one removed from your squad," Bridges said.

"I figured they would." He tried to hide his disappointment.

"Yeah, well, they also match with a slug that was taken from a victim found outside of La Joya." There was a pause, then Doug said, "Vic's name is Eduardo Martinez."

"Eduardo Martinez," he repeated, loud enough for Libby to hear. "Doesn't sound familiar."

"Sounds like Charlie Olson believes Martinez was a low-level player with the cartel. He was killed by a gunshot wound to the back of his head, allegedly by other members of the cartel."

It was more than they knew two hours ago, but not nearly enough. "Did Martinez live in La Joya?"

"No social security number on file for him, so we think he entered the country illegally. To be honest, we're not sure Eduardo Martinez is his real name. That was the name on a driver's license found on the body, but that's likely fake."

"Great," he muttered. "Not helpful."

"But we know for sure that the two gunmen who shot at you and Libby are connected to the cartel," Bridges pointed out. "Ballistics don't lie."

"Yeah." He knew police work was slow and meticulous. But it was different now that he was on the other end as a victim. "Interesting that the same gun is now here in Milwaukee, Wisconsin."

"Yep, they're a long way from Texas," Bridges agreed. "I'm glad you're tucked in the suite with Libby. I would recommend you order from the room service menu rather than risk going out."

"That's the plan." He considered asking Doug to arrange for a replacement vehicle, then decided against it. He'd left the truck parked near the side exit. There's no way the shooters could spot it by driving by.

Besides, Milwaukee was huge compared to Rio Grande City. He didn't think the cartel members would find it nearly as easy to navigate the streets here, the way they controlled the cities along the Texas and Mexico border.

"Olson seems concerned about Libby," Bridges said, interrupting his thoughts. "He mentioned she may need protection now that her brother has been murdered in prison. He told me that he drove by her apartment and saw how the place was trashed, then headed to the grocery store where she works during the summer. The store manager claims he hadn't seen or heard from Libby in the past three days."

"Yeah, well, Olson can stay in the dark about her being here in Wisconsin," Roscoe said firmly.

"I told him I had no idea where she was," Doug assured

him. "I gave him a story about cartel members here shooting each other to explain where I had gotten the slugs to put through the system. He seemed to take that at face value." There was a pause, then he added, "Trust me, I don't want anything to happen to either of you."

"Thanks for that." Roscoe was glad to know that Bridges was on their side. "Has Olson listed Libby as a missing person?" He hoped not because the additional media exposure would not help the situation.

"He said he wasn't listing her as a missing person at this point because her car is gone, and despite the destruction in her apartment, there was no blood found or other indication that she had been hurt. However, I suspect if there's no sign of her or the vehicle in the next day or two, he might report her as missing and in potential danger."

"I guess we'll cross that bridge when we come to it." He couldn't do anything about Olson reporting Libby as missing. The only thing that may work in their favor is that Texas was far away from Wisconsin.

"I plan to keep in touch with Olson, so if I hear anything more about that, I'll let you know," Bridges said.

"Great. I have Libby looking at mug shots of known cartel members to see if she recognizes any of them."

"I thought she didn't know what her brother was doing?"

"She didn't," he said quickly. "But that doesn't mean there weren't members of the cartel in the city. She worked at the grocery store and may have seen someone there."

"Anything is possible," Bridges agreed. "Keep me in the loop."

"I will. Thanks again." He ended the call, then crossed back to the table. "I know it's early, but we should probably order something from room service."

"I could eat," she admitted. "Although I'm not sure why I'm hungry while sitting and staring at a computer."

"We have a fridge and a microwave. Order enough that you can have something for later," he encouraged. He didn't like the idea of a pregnant woman going hungry. "That way you can eat whenever you like."

"Good idea." She scanned the menu. "I'll have the chicken wrap with fries. I can save half for later."

He placed the order for two chicken wraps with fries, then gestured to the screen. "No luck yet?"

"No." She frowned. "I'm sure this is a waste of time."

"Maybe, but we don't have anything else to do." He wasn't about to admit how much he would rather be out on the streets searching for the two gunmen than sitting and doing nothing. "I don't know if you heard that DEA Agent Charlie Olson went to your apartment and to the grocery store to find you."

"I caught the gist of the conversation." She shrugged. "I hated leaving the store in the lurch, but at least school is out for the summer. I would feel worse if I had to abandon my students."

He decided this wasn't the time to tell her she may not get a chance to return to her teaching job. Then he realized she would be delivering her baby in a few months and likely couldn't work anyway.

And how would she have supported herself? Would she really have kept the baby a secret from him?

There was a knock at the door. "Room service."

He crossed to look through the peephole. The man standing there stared down at the ground, as if not wanting his face to be seen.

When Roscoe didn't answer right away, the man

knocked again and spoke louder in a distinctive Hispanic accent. "Room service."

There were plenty of Hispanic residents in the city, but for some reason, he couldn't bring himself to open the door. Still watching through the peephole, the man pushed the tray aside and reached for his waistband.

"Look out!" Roscoe turned and threw himself in front of Libby as a spray of bullets pierced the door.

CHAPTER FOUR

Not again! Libby couldn't believe someone was shooting through the door! To her surprise, Roscoe curled his body around her, then awkwardly fired back at the door, three quick shots in rapid succession. He grabbed her arm. "Come with me," he whispered.

She wasn't sure what he had planned but went along with his pulling her to the bedroom farthest from the door. The sound of gunfire had stopped, but she was far from reassured. She worried that with enough bullet holes in the door, the shooter could easily gain access to the suite.

As if reading her thoughts, Roscoe went to the window and opened it. Then he pulled out a knife and cut through the screen. "You first," he said. "I'll help you."

She stared at the square window dubiously. "I won't fit through that."

"You will. But we need to hurry." He gestured to the windowsill. "One leg first, then duck through."

He made it sound easy when it wasn't. She threw one leg over the windowsill, then tried to duck her head to get through. The problem was that her belly made it impossible to bend forward far enough.

"Lean backward instead," Roscoe urged.

Scooting forward, she did as he suggested and managed to clear the window frame with her chin. Then she could angle herself outside the window to get the rest of her torso through. Thankfully, they were on the first floor of the hotel, so she could find the ground with the tiptoe of her shoe.

"Easy now." Roscoe held on to her as she struggled to get her other leg over the sill. Then she was standing there, shaking despite the warmth of the July sun.

In a heartbeat, Roscoe crawled through the window. He wrapped his arm around her waist, sweeping the area with his gaze. "We need to hurry. The truck is behind the hotel."

She nodded, picking up the pace. Getting away from the gunman was strong motivation. Despite her shaky knees, she walked quickly around to the back of the hotel. In the distance, she heard the screech of sirens.

"I'm sure the front desk clerk called it in," Roscoe explained. "But we're not sticking around."

"I understand." She would be more than a little relieved to get far away from this place. Even though she was beginning to wonder if she would be safe anywhere.

Roscoe wrenched the passenger door open, then surprised her by lifting her up and into the seat. Obviously, he wanted to be gone as badly as she did. She quickly pulled her legs in so he could slam the door shut. Seconds later, they were rolling away from the hotel.

At first he drove slowly, as if they weren't running away from yet another gunman. But when he reached the next street, he gave the truck more gas. He headed west, which made sense as there was only Lake Michigan to the east.

Several squads came roaring toward them from the other direction. Roscoe obediently moved over to give them room, then kept going. She twisted in her seat, watching as the police responders headed straight for the City Central Hotel.

Then she sagged against the door. "How did this happen?"

"I don't know." Roscoe's voice was curt. "I was assured that Bridges was clean. He and my team are the only ones who knew where we were staying."

She shivered again, still struggling to understand. "But Bridges made calls, right? Didn't he contact the DEA agent from Texas?"

"He did but promised not to reveal our location." Roscoe opened his window and tossed his phone out. She heard the device shatter on the pavement before he closed the window. "I'm not talking to anyone until I have a replacement phone. In the meantime, we need to find somewhere else to stay."

"Okay." Having zero knowledge of the area, she couldn't help him there. And tried not to cry when she realized her suitcase and his duffel had been left behind.

The only thing she really needed was the prenatal vitamins. She put her hands on her belly, struggling to remain calm. Missing a few days of vitamins wouldn't be the end of the world, but it was important to her that she follow her obstetrician's orders.

Which was ridiculous since she wasn't even in Texas anymore. And not likely to be heading back to his office for a routine checkup anytime soon.

She noticed Roscoe visibly relaxed after fifteen minutes of driving. He offered a reassuring smile. "We're good. I haven't seen anyone behind us."

For now. While she didn't say the words out loud, she knew Roscoe felt the same way. Like they were walking on eggshells waiting for the other shoe to drop. She'd barely had time to grieve over losing her father, and now her brother while being on the run for her life.

Things like this didn't happen to normal people. Then again, her brother had been working for the cartel.

Why, Tony, why?

There would be no answer.

"We need a clean vehicle," Roscoe said. "I don't want to leave a paper trail, though, so renting isn't an option."

She forced herself to concentrate on the situation at hand rather than wasting time and energy wishing things were different. "You're not going to steal one, are you?"

"No." He nodded thoughtfully, then added, "But I can do the next best thing."

She was almost afraid to ask. "Like what?"

"Change the license plate." He shot her a sideways glance. "It won't hold up under close scrutiny but should buy us a little time."

That didn't sound too dangerous, so she nodded. "Whatever you think is best."

He reached for her hand. "I'm sorry. I should have asked you to keep the vest on."

"It's fine." She shrugged, gripping his hand tightly. If she had to be stuck with anyone through a time like this, she was grateful it was Roscoe. He may have used her to get to her brother, but she didn't doubt that he would protect her with his life. "I wouldn't have gotten through the window while wearing it anyway."

"I would feel better if we had it handy, though. I still can't believe we were found at the hotel." His features hardened into a mask. "I'll eventually have to reach out to Rhy or

Joe. They'll hear about the shooting and will be concerned about us."

"I know you trust them." She stared at their clasped hands for a moment. "But I would feel better if we stayed on our own."

"I understand where you're coming from, but I'll need more cash soon and eventually a new set of wheels." He surprised her by lifting her hand and kissing it. "If I ask Rhy not to talk to anyone else, he won't. Same with Joe."

"Okay." She didn't see an alternative as she didn't have much cash with her either. She'd spent most of it along the trip here from Texas.

"There's a big box store," Roscoe said with satisfaction. He released her hand, and she felt adrift without his support as he exited the interstate. She folded her hands in her lap to keep from reaching out to him. "We'll get a pair of disposable phones there. Then I need to find black electrical tape."

The two stops took forty minutes. After acquiring the tape, Roscoe drove for another fifteen minutes before pulling off at a park and ride to work on the license plate. She climbed out to watch, amazed at how easily he was able to change the number 3 to an 8 and the letter P to an R. Even from a few feet away, she couldn't tell that the plate had been tampered with. It looked real to her.

As long as the tape held. She frowned. "I hope it doesn't storm."

"Tell me about it. That's why this is only a temporary fix." He rose and stuck the roll of tape in his pocket. "But it should be okay for the next twenty-four hours or so. There's no rain in the immediate forecast. And I feel better having some anonymity."

"Good." She rubbed a hand over her belly. "I'm hungry. We never got our dinner."

"We'll have to stop at a restaurant since the types of motels that take cash don't have room service." He shot her an apologetic look. "I'll do my best to find a place with connecting rooms, but there is no guarantee they'll be available."

"I know. It will be fine." Practically living with Roscoe would not be easy. She was already having trouble forgetting what it was like to have him hold her. Kiss her. And yes, make love to her. She had been emotionally distraught over her father's passing, but she had known what she was doing. And had not stopped him.

Despite Roscoe's asking her if she was sure.

She had hoped they had a future. But that was before he'd arrested her brother. Maybe it was time to stop blaming Roscoe for the situation they were in. He was in as much danger as she was and had done everything in his power to protect her.

Besides, staying angry with him would not help the situation. Just the opposite. She needed Roscoe now more than ever.

She rested her hand on her belly. Their child did too.

ROSCOE PULLED into the parking lot of a family restaurant that was roughly thirty miles outside of Milwaukee. He had not seen anyone following his black truck but did not relax his guard.

The incident at the City Central Hotel had been far too close. He'd felt the bullets whizzing past his head and could only thank God that he and Libby hadn't been hurt.

He chose the closest parking space, then killed the engine. Jumping out, he went around to help Libby.

"Thanks." She grimaced. "This truck is not made for expectant mothers."

"Sorry about that." He wished he'd have gotten rid of his truck. But then again, he hadn't expected Libby to show up pregnant either. "When we can, I'll swap for an SUV."

She waved a hand. "Don't mind me. I'm just tired."

No surprise there. He felt terrible that she'd been dodging bullets since the moment she arrived in Milwaukee. Literally on the doorstep of Cam's house.

The restaurant was relatively busy, but he was glad to see that there was a booth near the back that was available. At first the hostess seemed put off by his request to sit there, then shrugged and turned to lead the way.

He scanned the patrons, more out of habit than anything. There was no way the cartel could know they were at this specific restaurant. He wanted to know if the shooter had been caught or if he'd gotten away.

But that would have to wait until he found a motel and could get their new phones up and running.

One step at a time, he reminded himself. Feeding Libby was his priority. Along with keeping her safe.

He could not fail her and their baby.

"Can I get you anything to drink?" their server asked.

"Lemonade," he and Libby responded at the same time, making Libby laugh.

"Coming right up." The woman left them with their menus.

"There's barbecued spareribs," he said, breaking the silence. "They're not as good as back home, but they're not bad."

"Unfortunately, I have heartburn these days. Sometimes even lemonade is too much for me." She glanced down at the menu. "I'd like the pot roast."

"Sounds good." He sat back in the booth, eyeing her wearily. The adrenaline crash was always difficult. "I owe you an apology. I keep breaking my promise to keep you safe."

"There's no need to apologize. I'm only alive because of you," Libby said in a low voice.

It would have been easier if she'd stayed angry with him. "I'll do better from now on."

She shook her head but didn't say anything as their server arrived with their lemonade. "May I take your orders?"

"Yes, I'll have the pot roast with mashed potatoes," Libby said.

"I'll have the barbecued spareribs." Roscoe handed her their menus. "Thank you."

"Coming right up." The server hustled off.

"Roscoe, I'm grateful for everything you've done." She leaned forward, resting her elbows on the table. "I just wish I knew when this will be over. At some point, I need to see my doctor."

"I know." He'd wanted to ask her more about her pregnancy. He'd already done the math and knew she was due early October, but he wanted details. Did she have any ultrasounds? Blood tests? Was there anything to worry about? Did she know the baby's gender? It was frustrating to know he'd missed those first few months of discovery but told himself to be grateful she'd sought him out when she had.

"I'm fine, healthy as a horse," she said, reading his mind. "But I'm supposed to see the OB once a month. And it's already been two weeks since my last appointment."

"I'll find a way to get you back to Texas in two weeks," he promised rather rashly. Texas was the last place she should be, but if there was a way to make it work, he'd find it. "Try not to worry about that."

"I won't. It's more important to stay alive."

The statement hit hard. "I know. I'm sorry." He scrubbed his hands over his face. "If I could go back . . ."

"Don't." She sighed. "I've wasted enough time wishing things were different. We can't go backward, Roscoe. What's done is done. We can only move forward."

She was right. But that didn't make it easier to accept.

Their food arrived a few minutes later. After their server left, he stretched his hand across the table in a peace offering. She took his hand, then bowed her head. "Dear Lord Jesus, we thank You for this food we are about to eat. We also thank You for keeping us safe in Your care. Amen."

"Amen," he echoed, reluctantly releasing her hand to reach for his fork. He had prayed more in the past few months than he ever had in his life. His adopted parents had taken him to church, but he hadn't really gotten the message the way he had since joining the tactical team. And now Libby was praying too.

"This is really good," Libby said, after sampling her beef. "I'm surprised Yankees can do a good pot roast."

That made him chuckle. "I'm glad it meets your high standards."

They ate in silence for a few minutes. He found himself patting his pocket, only to remember he'd tossed his phone.

It felt strange not to be in communication with his team. With anyone, for that matter.

Not good to be so dependent on a cellular phone, but then again, it wasn't as if there were landlines or phone booths aplenty to use in lieu of having one. The moment they finished eating, he hoped to pay the bill and find a motel. He'd use street signs and billboards rather than his truck's GPS system.

When it was time to leave, Libby gestured to the restrooms. "I'll be back in a minute."

"No problem." He followed her to the alcove and stood near the door, determined not to let her too far out of sight.

They left the restaurant and settled in the car. The sun was slowly dipping behind the horizon as he pulled away from the curb. He stopped at the nearest gas station to fill up the tank, then he took the closest interstate ramp to keep heading west. He was getting low on cash, having just enough to convince some lowly motel clerk to give them a couple of rooms for cash. It would be imperative to speak with Rhy or Joe soon. "Keep an eye out for motels with vacancy signs. Hopefully, we'll find something despite the summer tourist season."

"The opposite of Texas, huh?"

"Exactly." No one wanted to visit Texas in the middle of summer. The glimpse of a sign caught his eye. "The Wildflower Motel is five miles away."

"That works." She craned her neck to see better. "I can't tell if their vacancy sign is on."

"Pray they have at least one room." The alternative to a motel would be sleeping in the truck, and he doubted that would be comfortable for Libby in her condition.

"We're in luck. The sign says vacancy," Libby said, after he exited the interstate.

"Great. Stay here, I'll arrange for the rooms, if they have more than one." He shifted the truck into park and shut down the engine. "I hope they're decent."

"Can't be any worse than the ones I stayed in on the way up from Texas," she said with a sigh.

He headed inside. To his relief, the middle-aged woman behind the desk brightened when he walked in. "You looking for a room?" she asked hopefully.

"I am." He showed her his badge. "I need two connecting rooms if you have them. And I would like to pay cash."

"Cash?" She looked taken aback, but then shrugged. "Sure, that's fine. But I only have rooms with two beds, no connecting rooms."

"I'll take one room, then." He pulled out his wallet. "How much?"

She named a figure that was more than reasonable.

"No paperwork, okay?" he said, pushing the cash and a tip toward her. "I'm protecting a witness."

"Sure, I understand." The woman scooped up the cash as if worried he would snatch it back. "Always happy to cooperate with the police."

"Thanks." He took the room key and turned away. Then he swung back to face her. "One more thing. I'd like to park my vehicle out of sight."

"Anywhere behind the building is fine," she said, slipping the money into her pocket. "Don't block the dumpster."

"I won't. Thanks again." He hurried back out to where Libby waited. He slid in behind the wheel and handed her the key. "Only one room, sorry, but there are two beds. It's the best she could do."

"Okay." Thankfully, she didn't look upset. "One thing about being pregnant is that I can sleep anywhere."

"Soon," he promised. "I'm going to drop you off at the room, then park this truck out of sight."

Ten minutes later, they were settled in a room that

wasn't as bad as he'd feared. Libby stretched out on the bed while he worked on the phones.

"I feel bad you had to leave your computer behind," she said with a yawn.

He shrugged. "The precinct will get it back, hopefully in working order." He was more concerned with the damage to the hotel room itself. His teammates had gotten the American Lodge shot up on occasion and made sure to pay for the repairs. He hoped Rhy would have the same philosophy this time.

Roscoe felt responsible, even if it was hardly his fault the cartel had found them at the City Central Hotel.

Doug Bridges must have been the leak.

"So tired," Libby whispered, tugging the blanket up. She turned away from him, and less than a minute later, he could hear her deep, even breathing, indicating she'd fallen asleep.

While he waited for the new phones to charge, he gazed down at her. Her long, dark hair was mussed, her expression relaxed.

"Sweet dreams," he whispered.

She didn't respond, already deep in slumber. Must be nice to fall asleep so easily. He had the feeling he wouldn't sleep well until the danger was over.

When the phones were fully charged and ready to go, he took one and carefully slipped outside, closing the door as softly as possible behind him so as not to disturb Libby.

Then he drew a deep breath and dialed Rhy's number. Good thing Rhy and Joe had insisted they each memorize each other's numbers. It wasn't smart to be completely dependent on a so-called smart phone.

Rhy didn't answer—no surprise as he was using an unknown number. He left a terse message, then did the same with Joe. He leaned against the wall, waiting for one of them to return his call.

A full five minutes passed before the phone vibrated. He quickly answered Rhy's call. "Hey, Rhy."

"What happened?" Rhy demanded.

"You tell me," Roscoe shot back. "I thought you said we could trust Bridges?"

"We can," Rhy said, a hint of concern in his tone. "I don't understand how you were found."

"Bridges came to the hotel; we met and discussed how to get information from the DEA agent I worked with in Texas. Guy by the name of Charlie Olson. Doug promised me he'd reach out to Charlie without giving away my location. Two hours later, a cartel member is knocking at the door, pretending to be our room service." He felt sick remembering how the bullets had punctured the door, narrowly missing them. "He fired several rounds, I returned fire, then took Libby out the rear bedroom window to get out of there."

Rhy whistled. "That's not good."

"No kidding." He tried to tone down the biting sarcasm. "Which brings us back to your brother's buddy, Doug Bridges."

"I'm telling you, Bridges is clean," Rhy insisted. "The guy has proven himself worthy, getting shot last year about this time while helping my brother Quinn and his wife, Sami, escape a drug cartel."

"Then explain to me how this happened?" Roscoe was suddenly very tired. "Because I know you and Joe didn't leak our location."

"Thanks for that," Rhy said in a low voice. "You're relatively new to the team, but I promise that we would never compromise one of our own."

"Yeah, I know." He rubbed the back of his neck. "But then how?"

"We're working on that. I'm leaning toward Charlie Olson being the leak. He knows you, Roscoe, and that you're a cop. When Bridges contacted him, he may have assumed Bridges was in contact with you. I'm sure the DEA has the resources to track your phone."

"I considered that possibility. I ditched my phone and will be using this throwaway from now on." He paused, then said, "I'm going to need support, Rhy. I've taken some measures to make sure my truck license plate isn't easily traced, but I'm running low on cash. I used up most of what I have on this motel room."

"That's not a problem. We're here for you, Roscoe." Rhy was silent for a moment, then said, "I'll send Jina and Zeke out with a replacement vehicle and more cash. Do you need anything else?"

"Maybe a computer, I left the one I took from the precinct behind in the suite. There wasn't time to grab it. The vest I'd borrowed for Libby is there too."

"Done," Rhy said without hesitation. "Do you want this stuff tonight or in the morning?"

He considered that for a minute. He believed they were safe here, and he was loath to wake Libby. "Tomorrow morning is fine. Maybe they can meet us someplace for breakfast. There's no room service here, and I know Libby will be hungry."

"That's not a problem. Oh, but there is one more thing you should know," Rhy said.

He tensed and straightened. "What's that?"

"You managed to hit the shooter at the hotel; he's at Trinity Medical Center in critical condition."

"I did?" That was the first break in the case they'd had

since this mess started. "Do you have a name? Known affiliations?"

"His ID lists him as Manny Corte, but we don't know if that's his real name or not," Rhy said. "His prints didn't show up in the system, so he could be here illegally."

It was a similar scenario to the murder of another suspected cartel member. "According to Doug, Charlie Olson said there's a guy by the name of Eduardo Martinez who was killed in La Joya. It's possible he had connections to the cartel too."

"We'll add him to the list. The good news is that Corte is still alive. Undergoing surgery as we speak. We'll question him as soon as we're able. The local police will want your weapon to match ballistics. I told them we'd get it to them when we could."

He wasn't giving up his gun anytime soon. "Thanks." It was sad that knowing he'd nearly killed a man was the best news he'd gotten all day.

He'd gladly take the thread of hope. Anything to be one step closer to keeping Libby safe.

CHAPTER FIVE

When Libby awoke, she blinked in confusion in the early morning light, not recognizing her surroundings. After a momentary flash of panic, she remembered coming to the Wildflower Motel with Roscoe.

Hearing Roscoe's deep, even breathing from the other bed made her smile. Then the baby kicked her bladder. Moving as softly as possible, she slipped from the bed and ducked into the bathroom.

After taking the opportunity to wash up, she ran her damp fingers through her hair. It wasn't the hot shower she'd have liked, but it was better than nothing. When she emerged a few minutes later, Roscoe was up and making coffee in the small four-cup pot the motel provided.

"Good morning." He greeted her with a smile. For the first time since she'd arrived, Roscoe looked like the sweet, teasing cop she remembered.

But maybe that was just a façade, not the real guy.

"Good morning." She forced a smile. "I tried not to wake you." She glanced at the coffee pot with longing.

"No worries." He gestured to the pot. "This is decaf for you. I'll make the real stuff next."

Touched by his kindness, she tried to smooth out her wrinkled clothing. Even sleeping fully dressed hadn't stopped her from conking out. "Sorry to fall asleep on you like that."

"Don't apologize, you need your rest." His expression turned somber. "I spoke to Rhy last night. We have a couple of new leads on the case."

"Tell me." She wasn't a cop, but she wanted to be kept in the loop as to what was going on. After all, she was the target here.

"The bullets pulled from Cam's house and my squad came from the same gun that was used to kill a man named Eduardo Martinez in La Joya." His gaze seemed to bore into hers. "Does that name sound familiar?"

"Not at all." She wished it did. "Do they think Eduardo is part of the Mexican cartel?"

"That's a strong possibility. However we don't know for sure that's his real name." Roscoe shrugged as he poured her a cup of decaf coffee. "You know how easy it is to get fake IDs."

"Yeah." She accepted the coffee. "I'm not sure how that helps us."

"I'm hoping to find out more about Eduardo Martinez." He began to make a second pot of coffee. "The other news is that I apparently injured the gunman who shot through the door at us. His name is Manny Corte; although again, that's the ID he was carrying, which may or may not be real. He's currently being treated at Trinity Medical Center."

"It's good to know he's still alive." She searched his gaze. "You think he'll talk to your boss about who hired him?"

"I hope so. But he's not in any condition to talk yet. He had surgery to remove the bullet and debris from the door from his abdominal wound." A shadow crossed Roscoe's blue eyes, making her think he didn't like having to use lethal force. Some of her anger and resentment toward him for using her to arrest her brother faded. Holding a grudge wasn't healthy. She had to believe God had done all of this for a reason.

"That is reassuring," she murmured.

"Yeah." He offered a half-hearted smile. "Maybe later today or tomorrow he'll be coherent enough to talk."

"What are we doing to do in the meantime?" She sipped her decaf, thinking that sitting in the motel room all day would be difficult.

Roscoe filled his cup with real coffee and then sat beside her on the edge of the bed. "I've arranged for two of my teammates to meet us for breakfast. They're going to bring a computer, a clean vehicle, and cash." He frowned. "I should have asked them to bring you some prenatal vitamins too."

"It's okay." She was keenly aware of him sitting so close. She stared into her coffee cup for a moment to get her bearings. What had he said? Oh yes, vitamins. "I—uh, doubt that missing a day or two is going to cause a problem."

"I know we need to pick up some more clothes for you too," he went on. "I feel bad you had to leave your maternity things behind."

"It's fine." She rose to set her coffee cup down, turning to face him. "I need to thank you for saving my life."

"Don't." His tone was hard, his brow furrowed. "This is my fault. If I hadn't arrested your brother . . ."

"He'd still be bringing drugs across the border and putting innocent lives at risk with distributing that poison," she interjected. "Arresting Tony was the right thing to do."

She only wished he'd truly cared about her, the way he'd pretended. "Besides, someone was going to throw him in jail him eventually. You said you were asked to come down from San Antonio to help the DEA. If not you, then someone else would have made the arrest."

"Yes." He held her gaze for a long moment. "I wouldn't have met you if I hadn't agreed to help the local police out."

And we wouldn't be expecting our child, she silently added.

"I don't think I mentioned my mother was a drug addict. She overdosed on heroin in the car when I was two and in a car seat." Roscoe cleared his throat. "She died, and I was put into foster care because my mother and her sister, Cam's mom, had lost touch. Thankfully, the Turners adopted me, and when I was sixteen, I discovered I had a cousin named Cameron. But I can't lie, my mother's drug overdose was part of the reason I agreed to help the DEA."

"I appreciate you telling me." His motive was understandable, yet she couldn't help feeling betrayed.

A long silence fell between them, eventually broken by the sound of a cell phone. She glanced around for the device, remembering that he'd stopped at the big box store to get a pair of cheap phones.

"This is my teammate," he said, pulling the phone from his pocket. "Hey, Jina."

She couldn't hear the woman's voice on the other end of the line but saw him nodding in agreement with whatever she was saying.

"That's great, thank you. I appreciate you grabbing that for us." Another brief pause, then he said, "If you don't mind, I'd like to meet at the family restaurant we stopped at last evening for dinner." He went on to give her the name and directions.

Libby had a feeling he was stopping for breakfast for her sake.

Roscoe glanced at his watch. "Sure, forty minutes sounds good. See you and Zeke then. Thanks." He ended the call, stuffing the phone back into his pocket. "Breakfast in forty if you can wait that long."

"Sure." The coffee wasn't sitting well in her stomach, but she managed to smile anyway. "Jina and Zeke?"

"Yeah. I work with a team of eight, led by Lieutenant Joe Kingsley and Captain Rhy Finnegan. You met Joe and Rhy yesterday."

She remembered the kind and considerate men clearly. "They seemed to care about keeping us safe."

"They're the best," he agreed. "Working on this tactical team has been a great experience. I've never experienced this much teamwork and camaraderie before."

She could tell that by watching him interact with them. Was this his way of letting her know he had no plans to move back to Texas? She tried not to show her dismay. "I'm glad you have friends you can trust."

"Friends *we* can trust," he corrected, rising to his feet. "These are cops who will put their lives on the line for you, Libby. The same way I will."

She stared at him, his words sinking deep and a wave of responsibility hitting hard. "I don't want anyone to die for me," she protested. But even as she spoke, her baby kicked and turned in her belly, reminding her there were two lives at stake.

Roscoe was right. She had to survive.

For their baby's sake.

"HEY, Libby, no one is going to die," Roscoe said, wishing he had the right to pull her into his arms. "We're highly trained police officers."

She nodded, but the way she smoothed her hands over her stomach betrayed her distress. Why hadn't he kept his big mouth shut?

He stepped closer, capturing her hands in his. "I promise we're going to get through this. I'm confident we'll figure out who is behind these attacks."

"I believe you." Her voice was a mere whisper as she gripped his hands tightly. "I believe God is watching over us."

"Good. I believe that too." He pressed a quick kiss to the top of her head. "We'll need to head out soon. Is there anything you need before we go?"

"Just another bathroom break." She drew a deep breath and released his hands. Sidestepping around him, she disappeared into the bathroom.

He jammed his fingers through his hair, then glanced up at the ceiling. Everything he'd learned about God and faith had been from his teammates. His adopted parents had attended church, but that practice had fallen to the wayside until he'd relocated here to Milwaukee. He would need all the strength and wisdom God could provide to keep Libby and their baby safe.

Turning, he crossed the room to glance out the window. The parking lot of the Wildflower Motel was empty except for one rusty sedan. The same vehicle that had been parked in front of door number two last night.

They had been safe here, but he had no intention of sticking around for another night. Especially since he still had his truck. Altered license plate or not, he wouldn't be satisfied until they had a clean vehicle and were settled in a new location.

He fully intended to keep his promise to keep Libby safe. Yet he also knew better than to underestimate the Mexican cartel. He wanted to believe Charlie Olson was the leak within the DEA, but having proof would be nice.

And nearly impossible to do from Wisconsin when Olson was in Texas.

"I'm ready."

He spun from the window at the sound of Libby's voice. "Great. I'd like you to stay here while I bring the truck around to the front."

"Okay." Her smile didn't quite reach her eyes.

He forced himself to leave, slipping out the motel room door and scanning the surrounding area as he made his way down past the row of rooms to the far corner where he'd parked his truck. It only took a minute to drive up to the door of their room. He pushed out of the driver's side door, intending to help her up, but somehow, she managed to grab the overhead handle to lever herself up and into the seat.

"I asked for an SUV." He glanced at her as he pulled away from the Wildflower Motel. "Hopefully, that will be easier for you."

"I can't imagine how women who are further along in their pregnancy manage to get into trucks like this," she groused as she fastened her seatbelt. "I guess if you're tall enough, it's not so bad."

"Do you know if the baby is a boy or a girl?"

"No. I told the doctor I wanted the gender to be a surprise." She glanced at him, then added, "I don't care if the baby is a boy or a girl. I only want our baby to be healthy."

Our baby. He had to clear his throat at the wave of

emotion that washed over him when she'd included him in that comment. When he could speak, he said, "I agree, that's the most important thing."

"Oh, I'm sure you want a boy, the way all men do," she said with a sigh. He remembered how she'd mentioned her father had always favored Tony over her. The night they'd spent together, she'd lamented the fact that she hadn't worked harder to mend her relationship with her dad.

And that now it was too late.

"That's not true," he said quickly. "I don't care if the baby is a boy or a girl. The only reason I asked is because calling the baby he or she would be easier."

"I know." She was smoothing her hands over her belly again. "There are times, especially once this all started, that I wished I hadn't canceled the ultrasound appointment."

"Surprises are more fun." He kept an eye on the rearview mirror as he took a very long and winding path to the restaurant, making sure they weren't followed.

Libby didn't say anything more as he finally pulled into the parking lot of the restaurant. He noticed two black SUVs sitting side by side and figured Jina and Zeke were already here. Just knowing that two of his teammates were close by eased his tension.

He was confident in his training and ability to keep Libby and their baby safe. But those horrible moments when he'd realized their room service attendant was a member of the cartel seconds before the guy had started shooting were far too fresh in his mind.

"Wait for me," he told her as he killed the engine.

As she unbuckled her seatbelt, he slid out and went around to offer his hand. She accepted it and managed to slide down from the elevated truck seat. Shielding her as best he could, they headed inside.

Standing in front of the hostess stand, he scanned the crowd, quickly picking up Jina and Zeke sitting in a booth within a direct line of sight to the door.

"We're with them," he said to the hostess as she pulled two menus from the stack.

"Of course. This way, please." She took the lead.

Zeke and Jina didn't look the least bit surprised to see a pregnant Libby walking toward them. Rhy had obviously briefed the entire team on Libby's precarious situation.

"Libby, this is Zeke Hawthorne and Jina Wheeler. Zeke and Jina, this is Libby Hall."

"Nice to meet you." Zeke offered his hand, then Jina did the same. Jina lifted a questioning brow but thankfully didn't say anything.

"Thanks for helping me—er, us out." Libby scooted into the booth.

"I understand it's been a difficult twenty-four hours for you," Jina said with surprising sympathy. Not that Jina wasn't a great cop, but the team's sharpshooter wasn't known to be soft and squishy. She was more hard angles and edges.

It was his turn to eye her with surprise, but Jina ignored him.

"By the way, we were able to grab your things from the City Central Hotel," Zeke said. "I have your duffel, the pink suitcase, and the computer."

"Oh, that's great, thanks." The way Libby smiled at Zeke made him grind his teeth together.

Then he silently lectured himself to knock it off. Libby was carrying his child, and Zeke knew better than to poach another guy's girl.

Okay, technically, Libby wasn't his girlfriend. At least, not anymore.

But he had high hopes she would be. Because whether she liked it or not, he was sticking close, even after the danger was over.

"Coffee?" A harried server crossed over holding a pot of steaming brew.

"Yes, please," he said, while Libby shook her head.

"No, thank you. But can I bother you for a glass of milk?" Libby asked.

"Of course, no problem." Their server took her request in stride. "I'll bring that back shortly."

The moment the server left, he leaned his elbows on the table. "Has anyone been able to question our perp at Trinity Medical Center?"

"Not yet," Zeke said. "Unfortunately, Corte is in the intensive care unit on a breathing machine. The surgeon did an initial surgery last night but left his abdominal inci-sion open." Zeke grimaced as if imaging how much that would hurt. "They're doing something called a staged abdominal repair procedure, which is basically going in every few days to clean him out. Sounds like they're worried about infection due to the door debris that entered his wound."

Roscoe sighed. "I wouldn't have shot through the door if he hadn't started it."

Jina barked out a laugh. "Obviously, it's all his fault."

"Yeah, it is." He sat back in his seat. "Okay, so getting information from him directly isn't going to happen anytime soon. Do we know anything else? Did they find his car or anything else that might lead us to who hired him?"

"A stolen car was found in the parking lot of the City Central Hotel," Jina said with a shrug. "We're waiting to hear if the fingerprints inside match that of our perp."

It wasn't much. Yet it had only been roughly twelve

hours or so since the shooting, and these things took time. Even with Rhy bugging the lab, they would have to wait in line. This current situation wasn't the only crime going on in the city.

Their conversation came to a grinding halt as their server returned with Libby's milk. "Are you ready to order?"

They were. Once they had placed their respective breakfast orders, the server fetched another pot of coffee to refill their cups. Then she left them alone again.

He sipped his coffee, trying to come up with other avenues to investigate. The idea of heading back to Texas to find Charlie Olson still gnawed at him.

"I heard you have reservations about Doug Bridges," Zeke said, breaking the silence. "Rhy insists he's one of the good guys."

He glanced at Libby, then shrugged. "I'm well aware that Rhy and his brother Brady have vouched for him. It's just hard to ignore how a gunman showed up at the hotel a couple of hours after Bridges left."

"Interesting timing," Jina mused.

"Rhy wants you to know that Bridges understands your concern, but that he plans to continue working the case." Zeke held his gaze. "You didn't ask for my opinion, but I think it's critical that you figure out a way to work with Bridges, especially if this is related to a Mexican drug cartel."

"Easy for you to say," Roscoe argued. "You weren't dodging bullets in that hotel suite or forcing a pregnant woman to crawl out a window."

"I'm fine," Libby spoke up. "It was more that I had trouble fitting through the window than it being a dangerous endeavor."

"I hear you on the dodging bullets," Zeke agreed. "But

you should know that Bridges is gathering intel through the Drug Enforcement Agency, seeking information on Charlie Olson. Rhy seems to think Olson is the leak you need to be concerned with. Not Bridges."

Thoughts of Bridges and Olson working together on this had swirled in his mind all night. He'd managed to get some sleep, but not nearly enough as he'd have liked. He took another sip of his coffee, then pushed his cup aside. "Okay, tell me this. Why would Olson ask me to gather intel on Tony Hall, support me in facilitating his arrest, then turn around and try to kill me and Libby?"

There was a long moment as Zeke and Jina exchanged a glance.

"We don't have an answer for that," Jina admitted.

"Maybe Olson is working for a different drug cartel," Libby said.

He, Zeke, and Jina all stared at her in surprise.

She leaned forward, her expression earnest. "Hear me out. Maybe that same rival drug cartel wanted my brother out of the picture, so they got Charlie Olson to drag you down to Rio Grande City and convinced you to find and arrest Tony. Once that was done, they arranged for him to be killed, then took things a step further to set up our deaths to look as if they're revenge from the drug cartel Tony worked for."

There was a long moment as the three cops at the table digested that.

"She's brilliant," Jina said with a rare smile.

"That does explain why someone broke into your apartment, trashed the place, and left a knife in the table," he said slowly. "Cartels aren't known for their scare tactics. They're known to be brutal and ruthless killers."

"Maybe Olson knew Libby would reach out to you,

Roscoe," Zeke added. "And that was the perfect opportunity to send cartel members here to take you both out of the picture, permanently."

"Okay, that's one scenario." He couldn't deny the logic of Libby's and Zeke's conclusions. "But that doesn't mean I'm ready to set up another face-to-face with Bridges."

"You don't have to," Jina said. "We'll be your intermediary. At this point, we haven't given your new disposable phone number to anyone outside the team. Bridges doesn't know how to reach you either."

"You should know Bridges feels terrible about what happened at the City Central Hotel," Zeke added. "He wasn't at all happy to hear how close the gunman got to you. If you ask me, the shooting has only made him that much more determined to get to the bottom of this."

"That works." The arrangement had Rhy's and Joe's fingerprints all over it, but that was fine with him. The added precautions would help keep Libby safe.

And that was all he cared about.

The conversation turned to lighter topics as their server returned with their meals. Jina picked up her fork to dig in, then hesitated when she noticed Libby had clasped her hands together to pray.

"I'll say grace," Roscoe offered, even though he'd never done that before. He took Libby's hand and bowed his head. "Dear Lord Jesus, thank You for this food we are about to eat. And please grant us the strength and wisdom to keep Libby and her baby safe. Amen."

"Amen," Zeke and Libby echoed.

"Dig in," Roscoe added with a grin.

Jina simply nodded, then dug into her omelet. The entire team suspected Jina came from a troubled past, one that kept her from embracing God and faith. Cassidy and

Raelyn were closest to her, but even they didn't know exactly what had happened.

Not that Jina's past was any of their business. She might have a chip on her shoulder at times, but Jina was a highly valued member of the team.

And she put her life on the line, the same way they all did, without hesitation.

"Where are you headed next?" Zeke asked.

"I'm not sure, but we'll need a place that allows us to stay off the grid without being too far from the city." He missed having a smart phone that had search capability. The phones he'd purchased were only good for talking and texting. "The Fourth of July holiday is an added complication. A lot of motels are booked."

"I'll find something," Jina said, using one hand to thumb the screen on her phone.

It didn't take long for her to provide three options. He quickly memorized the motel names and addresses. "Thanks. Hopefully, one of these will work."

"If not, call us and we'll find something else." Zeke pushed a key fob toward him, along with a thick stack of cash. "Computer, duffel bag, and Libby's suitcase are already in the SUV closest to the restaurant. Oh, I couldn't grab the vest as slugs were embedded in it."

"That's okay." He would be glad to have the few items they'd brought along. "Thanks. I'll leave my truck here."

"Nah, I'll drive it back," Zeke said, wiggling his fingers for the keys.

He hesitated, then handed them over. "You may want to ditch it in a park and ride outside the city limits. I altered the license plates, but if Charlie Olson is our guy, he likely has access to my DMV registration."

"If you've altered the plate, I'll be fine." Zeke didn't look concerned.

When they finished their meal, Zeke insisted on paying the tab. By an unspoken agreement, the three cops stayed close to Libby as they exited the restaurant.

Roscoe used the key fob to unlock the door. Zeke and Jina stood guard as he opened the passenger door for Libby. She slid into the seat without difficulty. He closed the door, then nodded at his fellow teammates. "Thanks for everything. I'll be in touch."

"Your baby?" Jina asked.

"Yes." He could feel his cheeks flush with embarrassment. "I didn't know she was pregnant until she came here to find me."

Jina punched him on the arm, hard enough to make him wince. "Stupid of you not to check on her." With that, she turned and climbed into the SUV.

Zeke simply chuckled and hopped into his truck. Roscoe joined Libby in the black SUV. Both Zeke and Jina waited for them to leave before heading out.

"Your teammates are nice," Libby said.

"They are." He hit the interstate, heading for the first motel Jina had found. It was a place called the Amber Inn, and it wasn't that far from their current location. Far enough from the city and the upcoming fireworks celebrations, he hoped, that they'd have a vacancy.

They'd been on the road for about ten minutes when his phone rang. He quickly pulled it from his pocket. "Yeah?"

"It's Zeke!" Before his teammate could say anything more, the sound of gunfire echoed through the speaker. "Stay safe!" Zeke shouted hoarsely before the line went dead.

CHAPTER SIX

"Take the phone." Roscoe pulled the device from his pocket and held it out to her. "Call Jina."

"What's going on?" She took the phone. Then frowned. "I don't know the number."

"I'll give it to you." As he recited the number, she punched the digits.

To her surprise, Jina answered on the first ring. "Roscoe? What's up?"

"It's Libby. Hang on, I'll put the call on speaker." She fumbled with the phone. "Okay, Roscoe, talk to her."

"Zeke is in trouble. He called to warn me, and I heard the crack of gunfire." Roscoe's expression was grim. "I knew driving my truck was dangerous. Please find him, Jina."

"I will. But you stay far away, Roscoe. I mean it. We'll handle this." Jina didn't elaborate but simply ended the call.

A look of anguish filled Roscoe's face, and she understood how much he'd rather be backing up his teammate. But then a resolute expression settled on his features. "Charlie Olson must be dirty. Only a cop would have the ability to track my truck."

"I still don't understand how the truck was found if you changed the license plates," she protested. "How is that even possible?"

"I don't know. Maybe Charlie Olson knew enough to keep an eye on the members of the team. I trust Zeke and Jina, but maybe he had someone following them from a distance." He shook his head in disgust. "I hate knowing I've put Zeke and the others in danger."

She wasn't sure what to say to make him feel better. She had come here to ask for protection but had brought danger from Texas all the way to Milwaukee.

"We can try to go somewhere else," she offered. "Maybe a different state?"

Roscoe shook his head. "I can't do that. I can't walk away from this." His jaw tensed. "Living off-grid isn't as easy as it sounds, especially when you're about to have a baby."

"Okay, I was only trying to consider alternatives." She sighed and smoothed her hand over her stomach. "I don't want your friends to be hurt because of me either."

"Not you, the cartel. And Charlie Olson." He watched the rearview mirror in a way that set her on edge. As if he expected the shooter to show up at any minute. "I think it's odd that the shooter attacked my truck when there was only one person inside."

"He may have assumed I was hiding in the back." She looked at him. "Zeke's hair is darker than yours, but it would be difficult to notice that from a distance. Now if Jina was driving? They may not have taken the shot."

"Yeah, maybe." He continued putting distance between them and the restaurant.

She thought about the beautiful blond Jina, wondering how she'd gotten into law enforcement. There had been a sense of toughness about her, despite her gorgeous looks. For a moment, Libby had been jealous but quickly realized neither Zeke nor Roscoe had looked at Jina as anything but a fellow cop.

Telling herself not to be foolish, she focused on the issue at hand. She had no idea where they were headed, but Roscoe's phone rang before she could ask. She quickly plucked it from the cupholder in the center console and then placed the call on speaker.

"This is Libby answering Roscoe's phone," she said.

"It's Zeke." She momentarily closed her eyes on a wave of relief. "Wanted you to know I'm fine, but your truck has suffered some damage."

"I don't care about the truck," Roscoe said. "I'm just glad you're okay. What happened?"

"I don't know for sure, other than I caught a glimpse of a silver truck coming up fast behind me. I called you, then swerved to get off the interstate as gunfire rang out. I was able to shake him loose, but now I wish I'd have stayed put and encouraged him to come closer." Disgust dripped from his tone. "I hate knowing he got away."

"Don't be foolish," Roscoe said sharply. "You did the right thing."

"Doesn't feel right," Zeke groused. "I only saw one man behind the wheel; he opened his driver's side window to fire at me. That may be why I was able to evade him so easily—it's difficult to shoot and drive at the same time."

"That's interesting. Makes it seem like whoever is pulling strings behind the scenes didn't have time to replace the guy I put in the hospital."

"Exactly what I was thinking." There was a brief pause, then Zeke said, "Oh, I had to leave your truck at a park and ride. Jina picked me up."

"That's fine," Roscoe said. "But make sure the crime scene techs search for evidence."

"Will do."

"We're relieved you're both safe," she repeated. "And we are too."

"Glad to hear it. We're heading back to the precinct to discuss next steps with Rhy and Joe," Zeke said. "We'll let you know if we learn anything."

"Thanks, Zeke. Take care of yourself. You, too, Jina. Later." Roscoe nodded to indicate she should end the call.

"I'm happy to know they're both okay." She would have felt guilty if something bad had happened to either of them.

"Yeah, but I still don't like it," Roscoe muttered. "We need a lead on who these guys are and where to find them."

She had no idea how to help him do that. Other than maybe to look at mug shots again. But that task seemed a useless endeavor.

There had to be hundreds of criminals who'd been arrested for drug trafficking. Maybe even a thousand.

A wave of hopelessness hit hard. What if they didn't figure out who was doing this before she was due to deliver?

What if this nightmare continued even after her baby was born?

"Hey, try not to worry." Roscoe reached for her hand. His intuitiveness caught her off guard. "We're going to get through this."

"I know." She forced a smile. "I believe God will show us the way."

"Yes, He will." Roscoe continued holding her hand as he navigated the streets. "I think one of the motels Jina pulled up on her phone is off the next exit. Not the Amber Inn, but the other one."

"Great." Being in a new location would help. "There's no way we can be tracked there, right?"

"Right." He gently squeezed her fingers reassuringly. "We have the computer too. I'll see if I can dig into Charlie Olson a bit." He scowled. "He must be involved in this."

She wasn't sure what to think, especially since they'd been taking extreme measures to stay hidden.

As Roscoe took the exit, she saw the small sign for the Red Mill Motel. There was no sign of a red mill nearby, which was a disappointment. From what she could tell, the place looked similar to the Wildflower Motel. Same single-story setup, with parking spaces in front of the rooms. Here there were several cars, though, which indicated that they might be busier than the motel they left behind.

She hoped the Red Mill was clean and bug free. Anything else she could handle.

"I'm going to stop to see if they have rooms," Roscoe said. "There's a vacancy sign in the window, but there are also several cars in the lot. If they're full, we'll move onto the next one."

"Sounds good." Glancing around, the motel was located across the street from a gas station, which included a small convenience store. No restaurants clustered nearby, yet she had noticed a sign for a place called the Pine Cone. Craning her neck, she looked on the other side of the interstate and caught a glimpse of the restaurant.

"Stay in the car, okay?" Roscoe parked near the lobby doorway. "This shouldn't take long."

As he entered the building, she silently prayed there was a room available. She needed to use the restroom again and was already feeling stiff and sore from sitting in the car. After traveling all the way from south Texas to Milwaukee, she had assumed her long hours in a vehicle were over.

Apparently not.

True to his word, Roscoe returned in five minutes. From the relieved expression in his eyes, she assumed he secured a room. He slid in behind the wheel and handed her a key card. "We're in room seven. No connecting rooms, but this one has two beds like the last one."

"Great." She frowned when he left the parking lot. "We're getting groceries now?"

"Yes. I figure we should grab something easy for lunch." He shrugged, then added, "We might be able to head over to the Pine Cone for dinner and breakfast tomorrow, but I would like to save our cash reserves as much as possible."

"Of course. That's fine." She couldn't blame him for being cost conscious, especially knowing they needed to pay cash for their motel rooms. She almost asked how much he'd had to spend but held back.

It wasn't as if she had cash on her to chip in for expenses. Being a teacher didn't pay that well, and neither did the grocery store job. She had pulled the maximum amount allowed from the ATM prior to leaving Rio Grande City but had gone through that relatively quickly. She'd used her credit card for all the larger expenses.

And look how that had turned out? She'd led the drug cartel straight to Roscoe.

They purchased a few snacks and sandwiches from the convenience store. She'd suggested buying cold cereal, but Roscoe shook his head. "Baby needs protein, remember?"

Upon returning to the Red Mill Motel, she was glad to see the sheets were clean, and there were no bugs. Other than the one daddy longlegs spider hanging out in the upper corner of the bathroom.

She unpacked their groceries as Roscoe brought in her pink suitcase and his duffel bag. She decided to take the time to shower and change her clothes. At the rate things had been going, she didn't want to wait.

The hot water was amazing, and it felt wonderful to be wearing clean clothes and to have washed her hair. After using the blow dryer, she joined Roscoe.

Roscoe booted up the computer. The room had a small table and two chairs, along with a small fridge, barely large enough for the quart of milk, cans of lemonade, and turkey lunchmeat they'd purchased. Roscoe had put everything away while she'd changed.

"Your turn," she said lightly, dropping into the chair beside him. Roscoe nodded as he logged into the police database. "I can look at more mug shots," she offered. "If you think that will help."

"It will but give me a few minutes to look into this guy Manny Corte first." After a solid ten minutes of searching, he leaned back in his chair, jamming the fingers of both hands through his hair. "There are too many guys with the name Manuel Corte to know if I have the right one. I'll try again after I get a photo of our perp from Gabe Melrose, our team's tech expert." He worked the keyboard again for a minute, then turned it toward her. "In the meantime, you might have better luck with the mug shots."

"Okay." She went to work, carefully going from one photo to the next, trying to remember if any of these men had visited the grocery store in the past few years.

As if her memory was that good, she thought sadly. In truth, she had a better memory for her students than random strangers.

Roscoe took his turn in the shower, then paced the room. She'd heard him make a few calls but didn't pay much atten-tion to the one-sided conversation. After about thirty minutes of looking, a familiar face flashed on the screen. Her fingers froze on the keyboard as she struggled to recall when she'd seen this man. Not the grocery store, but at her school.

"Roscoe?" There was a slight tremor in her voice. "This man had a student in my class last year."

"He did?" Roscoe leaned over her shoulder. "His name is Juan Gonzales." He grimaced. "That's about as common as John Smith."

"His son is Josue Gonzales." She couldn't tear her gaze from the screen. "I had no idea his father had been arrested for dealing drugs, although it looks like that charge was from three years ago." She hoped that meant Juan Gonzales had cleaned up his act.

"There's a lot you probably don't know about the parents of your kids," Roscoe said. He took down Juan's date of birth and last-known address. "I can ask one of the Rio Grande City police officers for more information on him." He grinned. "Nice work."

"Thanks." She was glad to have been useful, but his comment about not knowing about her kids' parents was hardly reassuring.

Would the father of a twelve-year-old really attempt to kill her?

As she continued to click through more photos, she silently prayed that wasn't the case.

***

ROSCOE CALLED Zeke to request information from Gabe Melrose on Juan Gonzales. "I have his DOB and last-known address, along with his booking number," he explained.

"Hang on, I'll have Melrose call you," Zeke said. "I'm

still with your vehicle. There's a slug embedded in the truck bed that the techs are working to extract."

"Thanks." He disconnected and waited impatiently for Gabe to call. Glancing over Libby's shoulder, he noticed she was still searching through mug shots.

He was surprised she'd recognized anyone, although she had a good eye for detail. Back when they'd dated, she'd regaled him with stories of her students and the funny stunts they'd pulled. Now she was forced to accept the reality that some of her students had parents who were criminals.

It might be a stretch to assume this guy is part of the cartel. Better to double-check than to be wrong. Rio Grande City wasn't a large city, but with fourteen thousand residents, it wasn't that tiny either.

When his phone rang, he quickly answered. "This is Roscoe."

"Hey, it's Joe. I hope you and Libby are safe."

"We are, thanks to Zeke and Jina. I hate that Zeke was targeted, though. I know for sure someone within law enforcement must be involved. No one else could have found Zeke in my truck."

"I agree and have updated Doug Bridges on the latest attempt." Joe's tone was somber. "Apparently, he's been trying to reach Charlie Olson without success."

"Oh yeah? Maybe that's because Olson is here in Wisconsin," he shot back. "Telling his cartel members where to find us."

"That is possible. Bridges has gone up the chain of command within the DEA. He's currently working with Olson's boss, a guy who runs the entire south Texas Drug Enforcement Agency. His name is Craig Wilke."

Roscoe filed that name away for reference. "What does Wilke have to say about Olson dropping off the planet?"

"Not much yet, but he is taking Doug's concerns seriously," Joe said. "Anyway, I wanted you to know that Manny Corte is still in critical care and not able to be interviewed. However, we're planning to fingerprint him to see if we can find him in the system."

"That would be good." He hoped they could find something on the man who'd tried to kill Libby. "I need to talk to Melrose about another possible link to the cartel."

"Okay, hang on." There was a pause as Joe spoke to their tech expert.

"Roscoe? It's Gabe. What do you need?"

"I'd like anything you can dig up on a guy named Juan Gonzales." He went on to give the date of birth and other identifying information. "This may be nothing, but he did some time for minor drug dealing, and Libby recognized him as being the father to one of her kids. She's a schoolteacher," he added to clarify. "I'd really like to know if he has any connections to the Mexican drug cartels. I have some computer access here, but you're better at crossmatching perps with other criminals."

"Not a problem," Gabe agreed. "I'll get right on this. Joe told me your girlfriend is pregnant and these guys are trying to kill her. And you."

"Yes, and they took shots at Zeke as well." He squirmed a bit at how Gabe had called Libby his girlfriend. While he wished that was true, it also sounded lame. He'd rather introduce her as his fiancée. Or better yet, his wife.

Not that Libby would even consider that sort of relationship.

"Anything else?" Gabe asked, interrupting his thoughts.

"Not yet. I may need more information along the way,

though, so take down this number. We ditched our cell phones for disposable ones."

"Got it," Gabe said. "Stay safe, Roscoe."

"We will." He lowered the phone, sincerely grateful for the support of the tactical team. Support he wouldn't have if he'd stayed in Texas.

Sure, the police department in San Antonio had a similar camaraderie among the cops working there. But what he experienced here within Rhy's tactical team was different.

Better than most. There was no rivalry among the team members. General ribbing and teasing, yes. He'd done his fair share of joking around. But when push came to shove, they all had each other's backs.

"Roscoe? I found another familiar face." Libby's comment had him crossing over to join her. The man looking back at him from the screen had several facial tattoos, all appearing to have been done outside a professional tattoo parlor.

"How do you know him?"

She swallowed hard. "I'm fairly sure I saw him walking past my brother's apartment." She turned her head to look up at him. "Not very long ago, like while we were—uh, dating."

"Are you sure?" He rested his hand on her shoulder, wanting to believe her. But guys with lots of tattoos were plentiful in the area, and one could look like another.

"I am. It's this tattoo here that caught my attention." She pointed to the crude snake that was inked on his neck. "I am scared to death of snakes, having been bitten when I was young. I was horrified to see that he'd put a tattoo of a snake on his neck. As if the thing was choking him." She shivered. "I stared at it for a long time before he hurried away."

"Okay, I believe you." The guy's name was Pedro Alverez, and he had also done time for drug trafficking.

It was interesting how many of these guys were back on the street despite the drug charges brought against them. Which made him wonder if Charlie Olson had somehow helped them out.

How, he wasn't sure.

Libby's theory about two cartels, one that Charlie was working for and the other that Tony had been recruited into, was beginning to make sense.

"Why isn't he still in jail?" Libby asked, voicing his concern. "I don't understand how I could have seen him more than six months ago if he'd been previously arrested for selling drugs."

"I don't know." He quickly called Gabe Melrose back. "Hey, sorry to bother you, but I have another name for you to use in cross-referencing our perps." He gave Melrose Alverez's name and last-known address. Which, he noticed in surprise, was the same apartment complex Tony Hall had lived in.

No doubt in his mind that Libby had seen this guy. And worse, this guy had probably taken note of her too. A beautiful woman like Libby would catch any man's eye.

"Got it," Melrose said. "I'll add him into the mix."

"Thanks, Gabe. I'll look forward to hearing from you." He set the phone on the table. "Libby, do you mind if I take a turn at the computer?"

She nodded and rose, her expression troubled. When he caught a glimpse of tears in her eyes, he reached out to her.

"Hey, don't get upset over this." He was at a loss in dealing with her tears. "You did good work today."

"What if that man was working with Tony?" Her anguished green eyes clung to his. "I can't stand the idea that my brother would have brought drugs across the border with someone like him!" She waved her hand at the screen.

"Libby, please." He drew her close. "Try not to dwell on the criminal aspects of these guys." This was his fault for asking her to help. "All we want is a place to start looking for these creeps. But the rest of the team will do that while I stay here, keeping you safe."

"Oh, Roscoe." She slipped her arms around his waist and buried her face against his chest. "I wish . . ." Her muffled voice trailed off.

He cradled her close, thrilled to have her in his arms again after all this time. There were many things he wished, too, mostly that he hadn't left her alone in Texas.

Jina was right. He'd been an idiot not to check in on Libby before now.

She hugged him hard, then loosened her grip and stepped back. "Sorry. My hormones have been out of whack lately."

"Don't apologize." Using his thumb, he wiped away her tears. "I'm here for you, Libby. I feel terrible that you're in danger over this."

"Yeah, well." She sniffled and shrugged. "I've been wrong to blame you, Roscoe. Tony was the one who started this. I've held such a grudge against you for something that wasn't your fault. Especially hearing about how your mother died of an overdose."

"It was partly my fault." He held her gaze. "But please know that I never lied to you about my feelings for you."

She glanced away. "I want to believe that, but it's not easy. I always come back to the fact that if you hadn't been looking for information about my brother's possible criminal activity, we never would have met."

That was true. And her brother had lost his life because of it as well. "You said something important, Libby. That God brought us together for a reason." He placed his hand on her abdomen. "I have been learning about God and faith over the past few months. I believe God knew this baby needed his mother and father to be together."

She covered his hand with hers. He almost gasped out loud when the baby moved beneath their fingers. A soft smile curved her lips. "Feel that? This baby sure likes to kick. Maybe we have a future soccer player on our hands."

"I'd love that." He was touched by the way she'd included him in their future. As if they would have a future. All three of them, together.

Something he wanted more than he'd have thought possible.

"Libby, I—" his phone rang, cutting him off. With a sigh, he reached around her to grab it. Recognizing Joe's number, he wished his boss had better timing. "Hey, Joe. Please tell me you have good news."

"Sort of good news," Joe said. "I heard Libby has identified a few possible cartel members."

"Yes, but if you ask me, Pedro Alverez is a more likely candidate than Juan Gonzales," he said. "Gonzales has a son in her school."

"Well, that's rather interesting because Jina went to the hospital to get the gunman's fingerprints. Gabe just finished running them through the system. No surprise, the driver's license with the name Manny Corte was fake. His real name is Juan Gonzales. The same guy Libby identified."

"Wait, are you sure? Juan Gonzales?" He looked at

Libby who was close enough to hear the conversation. "You're positive they're one and the same?"

"Yep. Here, I'll send an email with his information so you can see for yourself." There was a pause as Joe worked the computer. "Check your email."

"Hang on." Pinching the small disposable phone between his ear and his shoulder, he logged into his email. Joe's message was at the top, and he quickly double clicked on the attachment.

The same mug shot Libby had found of Juan Gonzales bloomed on the screen.

Irrefutable proof a citizen from Rio Grande City had traveled several thousand miles to kill him and Libby.

And their unborn child.

CHAPTER SEVEN

"I can't believe it." Libby felt sick as she stared at the image of Josue's father on the screen. She'd heard enough of Roscoe's conversation to understand this man was the shooter at the City Central Hotel. And likely the same man who was in the truck that fired at her outside Cameron's house.

If anyone had told her a student's father would try to kill her, she wouldn't have believed them. Granted, she'd had Josue in her class the year before last, but she'd had parent-teacher conferences with this man. Had discussed his son's progress with him.

Now he'd come all the way to Wisconsin to kill her.

She sank into the closest chair, swallowing hard. The only part of this that was reassuring was knowing this man was in the hospital and couldn't hurt anyone again.

"I really need to know when this guy is awake and able to talk," Roscoe was saying. "It would be good to figure out who hired him."

Glancing up at Roscoe, she waited for him to finish the call, before saying, "I want to talk to Juan Gonzales too."

Roscoe's blue eyes narrowed. "Not happening."

"I know him," she insisted. "I had parent-teacher conferences with him. I might be able to use his son to get through to him."

Roscoe looked away, then shrugged. "We can't talk to him yet, so it's a moot point."

She knew he would try to wiggle out of allowing her to talk to Juan, but she wasn't going to drop the issue. They would be perfectly safe in the hospital, especially a critical care unit surrounded by people and medical staff.

She wanted to look into Juan's eyes to see—what? Regret? Shame? Anger? Hatred? Guilt?

None of the above? Maybe the devil only had emptiness in his eyes.

"You should keep looking at mug shots," Roscoe said, interrupting her troubled thoughts. "Your plan is working."

"It was your idea, not mine." She nudged him aside to draw the laptop closer. "But I'll gladly keep searching." When she minimized Juan Gonzales's photo, she saw the man with the snake tattoo. "What about this man?"

"I'm waiting for Gabe to get back to me about him." He sighed, and added, "I'm trying to be patient, but it's not easy."

"I hear you on that." She stared at the man's face, wondering again why her brother would have gotten mixed up with him.

Unless snake-tattoo guy hadn't given Tony a choice. Deep down, she wanted to believe her brother hadn't jumped at the chance to bring drugs across the border. That he'd only done it under duress. Her brother hadn't been a bad guy.

And he'd paid dearly for his sins.

"I feel bad I didn't get to talk to Tony," she said as she minimized snake guy's picture.

"About what?" Roscoe asked.

"I was pretty harsh with him over the arrest. Then I got angry with him for having our father sent to the funeral home and cremated before I could see him." She glanced up at him. "He said that it was better if I didn't see our dad because he had fallen on his face, and it was disfigured from lying on it until he'd been found, but I was still upset."

"I'm sorry, Libby." He reached for her hand. "I'm sure that was difficult."

She shrugged. "It wasn't like we had money for a funeral, so the cremation part was fine. I just . . ." Her voice trailed off. It was difficult to explain how horrible she'd felt not having the chance to say goodbye.

Her gaze dropped to her belly, remembering how Roscoe had held her the night she'd learned about her father's death. How they'd spent the night together.

How she'd fallen in love with him.

"I'm fine." She did her best to convince herself that those feelings weren't real. That they were based on a lie. Even though Roscoe had claimed to care about her, she couldn't ignore the fact that he'd only asked her out to talk about Tony.

Maybe he was right about God bringing them together, but that didn't mean she had to risk her heart again. He'd already broken it once. Foolish to allow round two.

Releasing his hand, she turned back to the keyboard. Enough wallowing in the past. That was nothing but a waste of time and energy. Time to stay focused on moving forward. Which included obtaining answers related to the danger that stalked them.

Clicking through the photos was tedious. Twice her

mind wandered, and she had to go back to review the images she'd managed to skip. After a quick bathroom break, she emerged to find Roscoe on the phone.

"That's good work, Gabe," he said, glancing at her as she approached. "I'm convinced Charlie Olson is involved in this."

A dirty DEA agent, she thought with a sigh. As if there weren't enough problems with illegal drugs entering the country, they had to contend with cops who took money to look the other way.

Or worse, facilitated the killing innocent people.

"What did he find?" she asked when he ended the call.

"Pedro Alverez, your snake-tattoo guy, was arrested, but then somehow the drug evidence that had been confiscated disappeared, so they had to let him go." His voice was laced with disgust. "How much do you want to bet that Charlie Olson had something to do with the disappearing drugs?"

"That's a possibility, but it's not proof Olson was involved," she protested. "Don't get me wrong, I believe he's dirty, but missing evidence isn't proof."

"The evidence was supposedly secured by the DEA," Roscoe said. "Only a DEA agent could take it out without anyone knowing."

"Don't they have checks and balances for that sort of thing?" It seemed highly unusual that any agent could walk in, take drugs, and leave.

"I don't know the details on how that evidence was taken, but Gabe mentioned discussing the various possibilities with Doug Bridges." He frowned. "I may have to talk to Bridges myself at some point. I wanted to keep him at arm's length, but it's hard to suspect him of being a bad guy when the entire Finnegan family vouches for him."

"Whatever you think is best." There was no reason to

second-guess Roscoe's intuition. Despite everything that had happened since she'd arrived in Wisconsin, he'd kept her safe. She trusted him implicitly when it came to sheltering her from danger.

It was her heart that she needed to protect.

"I'll give him a call later," Roscoe said. "Let me know when you need a lunch break."

Glancing at the clock, she was surprised to realize it was going on noon. She must have worked at the computer for longer than she'd thought.

"Let's eat now," she said. "I didn't take my prenatal vitamin yet and need to do that with food."

"Sounds good."

She rummaged again in her pink suitcase. Pulling out the vitamins, she dropped one horse-sized pill in her hand and then reached for the can of lemonade Roscoe offered.

He carried two sandwiches to the table. She sat beside him. "Let's say grace."

"Yes. We have a lot to be thankful for." He took her hand. "Dear Lord Jesus, we thank You for keeping us safe in Your care. Please continue to shelter our baby as we seek those who wish us harm. Amen."

"Amen." She was touched by his prayer.

It only took a few minutes to eat their simple sandwiches, but she wouldn't complain. The long afternoon stretched before them, though, which made her feel restless. Even in the summer months, when school wasn't in session, she didn't sit around all day. She worked at the grocery store, cleaned, took walks.

She went back to the computer when Roscoe's phone rang again. Considering his ability to investigate from here was limited, she was grateful those helping him were working overtime.

"Hey, Rhy, what's up?" There was a pause as he listened. "Really? He's awake? I thought he needed more surgery?"

She straightened, hoping he was talking about Juan Gonzales. Interviewing the man who'd tried to kill them had the potential to blow the case wide open.

If he could be convinced to cooperate.

"Libby wants to be there when we talk to him," Roscoe said, glancing at her. "I told her that wasn't possible, but she knows this guy from parent-teacher conferences with his son."

She jumped to her feet. "Let me talk to him."

Roscoe shook his head, but then frowned. "Are you sure that's a good idea?"

Had Rhy agreed with her request? She found herself holding her breath while she waited for Roscoe to finish the call.

"Yeah, okay. We'll be there in about forty-five minutes." Roscoe lowered the phone, his gaze resigned. "Rhy agreed that you should be included."

"That's wonderful." She impulsively threw her arms around him in a quick hug. "Thanks. I feel good about this, Roscoe."

"Yeah, well, that makes one of us," he muttered, hugging her back. Then he stepped away. "Let's hit the road. We need to talk to Gonzales before his condition changes for the worse."

"Is that a possibility?" She grabbed her purse from the bed and followed him outside to the SUV.

"Who knows?" He shrugged, opening the door for her. "The doc has listed his condition as critical but stable."

As she buckled her seatbelt, Libby prayed with all her heart that Juan would be able to speak with them.

And that she could help convince him to cooperate.

ROSCOE DIDN'T LIKE TAKING Libby along to interview Juan Gonzales, but he was anxious to speak with the shooter himself. Rhy had said it would be smart to use all the tools at their disposal to get through to Gonzales. The guy was a hardened criminal, yet he had a son. A boy he must have cared about to have attended parent-teacher conferences with Libby.

If he were honest, he'd admit it was a relief to get out of the small motel room for a while. Libby looked better than ever after she'd showered and changed. The scent of her shampoo was imprinted in his mind.

He'd wanted to kiss her.

Enough. He gave himself a mental shake. Time to focus on the case.

Keeping a wary eye on the rearview mirror, he was relieved to note there was no one behind him. Once he hit the interstate, there was plenty of traffic, but none that appeared to be following them.

He drove slowly in the right lane, where vehicle after vehicle either passed them or got off the freeway. Libby seemed lost in her thoughts as he drove. Since he was barely going above the speed limit, the trip seemed to take longer than usual.

Or maybe it was just that he didn't want Libby to be anywhere near the gunman who'd tried to kill them.

The traffic grew more congested as he approached the city limits where Trinity Medical Center was located. He glanced at her, then gestured to the impressive building housing the hospital. "I can drop you off at the front entrance," he offered.

"No need. Walking is good for me. I try to walk at least three miles a day."

"In your condition?" He frowned. "Not sure that's wise."

"My doctor says it's fine." She narrowed her gaze. "I wouldn't do anything to harm my baby."

So now it was her baby, not theirs. He let it go, navigating his way through the medical center to the parking garage. The place was packed, forcing him to go all the way up to the top floor.

If he remembered correctly, there were elevators they could use rather than hiking up and down the stairs. No matter what her doctor had said, he didn't think that was a good idea.

"Hang on," he cautioned when she hopped out of the passenger seat. "Let me call Rhy. He wants to meet us."

"That's fine." She lifted her face to the sun. "It feels good to be outside."

He made the call. "Hey, Rhy, we're up on the top floor in the parking garage."

"I parked up there, too, but am now in the waiting room. We have to call up to the ICU ahead of time, we can't just barge in," Rhy explained.

"We'll be right there." After pocketing the phone, he reached for Libby's hand. "Let's go. Rhy's waiting inside."

She fell into step beside him. If she was nervous about this upcoming interview, she didn't show it. Since he couldn't come up with a way to dissuade her, he let it go.

He was familiar with Libby's stubborn streak. It had been one of her personality traits that had been both admirable and annoying.

Today, it was annoying.

The hospital was teeming with people. As they approached the waiting room, there was a large desk that indicated they had to stop to be issued a visitor pass.

Decent security, he thought as they put their names on the list and clipped badges to their clothing. He saw Rhy waiting near the doorway when they were given permission to enter the room.

"I'm glad you're here. Give me a minute to call the nurse." Rhy moved toward another desk where a woman with a volunteer badge sat alongside a security guard. *Even more security*, he thought.

When Rhy finished, he turned back toward them. "We're cleared to go up to the third floor. Normally, prisoner patients aren't allowed visitors. Cops, yes; civilians, not so much. I had to go up the ladder within hospital administration to smooth the way for Libby to tag along."

He continued holding Libby's hand. "I can understand the hospital's reluctance to have lots of people visiting." He glanced at Libby who looked around curiously. "I hope this is a good idea."

"It can't hurt," Rhy said with a shrug. "I figure you and I will start the interview, and if we don't get very far, we can turn things over to Libby."

"I believe he'll recognize me as his son's teacher," Libby said. "He seemed to care about his son, so reminding him of that bond may encourage him to talk."

Roscoe had his doubts, but he didn't voice them. "Is Gonzales cuffed to the bed?"

"He is," Rhy said. "And there's an MPD officer sitting on him too."

He nodded, knowing the arrangement was the usual

procedure for prisoner patients. Even more so for a prisoner who tried to kill a cop.

The shrill beeping of alarms and sharp antiseptic scent assaulted his senses when they walked inside the intensive care unit. The place was chaotic with noise and people, some scurrying in a hurry while others were clustered around computer screens, discussing patient conditions.

Rhy approached the main desk to ask which room, but Roscoe had already noticed the uniformed officer standing outside door number three. He gestured for Rhy to follow him to the room.

"You can only have a few minutes," the nurse in blue scrubs warned them sternly. "Mr. Gonzales needs his rest."

"We understand," Rhy said. "We wouldn't be here if it wasn't important."

The nurse turned to double-check the IV pumps, then scooted past them, giving them a few minutes alone with Gonzales.

Rhy approached the patient's bedside. "Mr. Gonzales? I'm Captain Rhyland Finnegan, and this is Officer Roscoe Turner. We'd like to ask you a few questions."

Gonzales looked at them, then his gaze moved to Libby. Roscoe noticed Juan's eyes opened wider as he recognized his son's teacher.

"I can't talk to you without my lawyer," Gonzales said hoarsely.

"Mr. Gonzales, how is your son Josue doing?" Libby leaned over to take the prisoner's hand. It was all Roscoe could do not to physically lift her off her feet and carry her out of there. "He's a great student. I'm sure you must be proud of him."

Gonzales seemed to fixate on her for a long moment.

Then he closed his eyes as if he couldn't bear to see her. "I'm sorry," he whispered.

"Sorry you tried to kill me?" Libby moved closer, edging Roscoe out of the way. Her pregnant belly pressed against the side rail. "Did you know I'm pregnant? Are you so callous that you would kill an innocent woman and her baby?"

"*Madre de dios,*" he whispered. Then he opened his eyes to look at her. "I didn't want to hurt you, but I didn't have a choice. They threatened my son . . ."

"Who threatened him?" Roscoe asked urgently. "Tell us what's going on and we can help protect you and your son."

"He'll kill me." Gonzales shook his head, then winced. "Go away. I can't help you. I need to talk to my lawyer."

"We can get your lawyer here," Rhy said in a soothing voice. "I'll make the arrangements."

"I don't know . . ." Gonzales looked at Rhy but then back to Libby. "How can I be sure you'll protect my wife and son?"

"We're working with the DEA here in Wisconsin, and I give you my word we will do whatever is necessary to protect your family," Rhy said. "But only if you fully cooperate with us. Do you understand me? We need to know who hired you."

"The DEA?" Gonzales's eyes widened in abject horror. "No! I don't trust them! No DEA. I won't talk to them."

Juan Gonzales's visceral reaction only reinforced Roscoe's belief that Charlie Olson was involved in this. "Not Charlie Olson," he hastened to reassure him. "I promise you can trust our local DEA officer, Doug Bridges."

"No, no, no." Gonzales moaned, then suddenly his entire body went tense. Then it began to shake, his head turning to the side, his gaze staring blindly at the ceiling.

Overhead, his monitor beeped loudly. It looked to Roscoe's inexpert eye that Gonzales's heart rate had jumped into triple digits.

The nurse quickly rushed into the room, pushing past them. "What did you do?" she demanded.

"Nothing." Roscoe tried not to sound defensive. "He was talking to us, then he started to shake."

"He's having a seizure," she snapped. "I need you all to leave, now! Don't make me call security to escort you out of here."

A seizure? Roscoe didn't want to leave, but the nurse didn't give them a choice. He had no doubt that she'd call security to escort them out. Seemed the hospital was full of security guards, which was probably a good thing.

Rhy tugged on his arm. He reluctantly turned away with Libby.

More staff members ran in to help. Roscoe stood next to the uniformed officer with Rhy and Libby, taking care to stay out of the way of those who needed access to the patient. "Did you hear that? He's afraid of the DEA," Roscoe murmured.

"Yeah." Rhy glanced back at the room. "I can't believe he's having a seizure. He was so close to spilling the name of the guy who hired him."

"Maybe when this medical emergency is over?" Roscoe hoped the seizure wasn't serious enough to keep Gonzales from talking.

"I hope so. We can pray for him," Rhy said with a sigh. "For now, we need to leave. He should have his lawyer present when we talk to him again. I'll reach out to the guy. I know he's with the public defender's office."

"I hope Juan's lawyer will agree to work with us," Roscoe said, feeling only a little better about the situation.

"Wait, what if his wife and son are in danger?" Libby protested. "We can't just ignore what he said back there. We need to do something!"

"I promise we're not ignoring his family's plight," Roscoe assured her. He looked at Rhy. "Looks like we need to get Bridges here ASAP. Maybe he can reach out to a different DEA agent that can check into Josue's situation."

"Yeah." Rhy's expression was troubled. "I don't like knowing his son is in danger."

"I agree, although that doesn't give him the right to shoot at us." Roscoe felt bad for the guy, but attempting to kill Libby and her baby was inexcusable. If not for his paranoia in peering through the peephole, they could both be dead.

As much as he hated to admit it, bringing her along had been the right decision. She had clearly gotten through to Gonzales in a way he and Rhy hadn't.

"That's true." Rhy turned and led the way toward the main doorway. "Let's give them room to work."

They stepped outside the intensive care unit, into the main hallway. At first the area was deserted, then two staff members pushed a patient on a gurney past them.

"I need to call Bridges and Juan's lawyer," Rhy said. He led the way to a row of windows that wasn't far from the main elevators. "Let's stay here for a few minutes, it's crowded and noisy in the waiting room."

"Fine with me." He stood close to his boss, listening as he made the call.

A brown-skinned Hispanic man with a visitor tag stepped off the elevator, along with a few staff members, nurses or doctors, wearing scrubs. The staff didn't appear to be in a hurry, chatting away as the Hispanic man lingered behind them.

Roscoe wasn't sure why, but the guy's furtive actions caught his attention. Then his gaze dropped to his gloved hands.

Gloves?

Even as the realization sank deep, the man dipped his hand into his pocket, then pulled it out again. Seeing white powder, Roscoe didn't hesitate.

"Drugs!" He shouted so loud the hospital staff members abruptly stopped in their tracks, gaping at him. The move was so sudden, the Hispanic man bumped into them, the white powder flying up in the air.

He grabbed Libby and pulled her away from the cluster of people, holding her close to his side and pulling the end of his T-shirt up to cover her nose and mouth.

Behind him, he heard bodies falling to the linoleum floor with horrifying thuds.

Frantic now, he dug for his phone. But Rhy had beaten him to it, taking the same precaution of covering his nose and mouth to protect himself from whatever drug, likely fentanyl, had been tossed into the air.

"Drug overdose on the third floor outside the intensive care unit," Rhy shouted into the phone, his voice muffled by the shirt. "Send medical help immediately!"

Roscoe held his breath, doing his best to ignore the need to breathe as he scanned the area for the Hispanic man.

The perp who'd brought the drugs into the hospital was lying on the floor next to the hospital staff members, all of them appearing to be unconscious.

And if help didn't arrive quickly, they would die.

CHAPTER EIGHT

It was hard to breathe with Roscoe holding the cloth over her face, but Libby did her best to remain calm. He'd seen drugs, and she knew from the training they'd received at the middle school that some drugs, like fentanyl, could be transmitted through touch or breathing in the tiny drug particles.

Fentanyl was so powerful that even a very small amount could cause an overdose. And worse, death.

"Are you okay? Do you feel funny?" Roscoe asked, his voice tight with fear. "I want to get you down to the emergency department ASAP!"

"Fine," she managed to say. "Need to breathe, though."

He loosened his grip. She experienced a weird sense of wooziness but did her best to shake it off. It was probably her imagination more than a physical response.

The thud of pounding footsteps reached them. She turned to see a stairwell doorway burst open, revealing several staff members.

"Be careful," Roscoe warned. "I believe fentanyl particles are on the floor and maybe on their clothes."

The two females and one male looked shocked but

brought face masks from their pockets, then donned gloves. One of the females also pulled syringes from her pocket.

Likely Narcan, or so Libby hoped. During their training, they'd learned how to administer Narcan to save children suffering drug overdoses.

It made her think of Roscoe's mother, dying with her son in the back seat of her car.

"We need to get out of our clothes," Rhy said. "Good eye, Roscoe."

"Thanks. Yes, I want Libby to been seen in the ED," he said. "Maybe we can change there."

Rhy nodded, gesturing to the stairwell. "I know where it is, down on the first floor. My sister Alanna and my sister-in-law Faye Finnegan both work there." His expression darkened. "Faye is pregnant, so I hope she stays far away."

"Show us where to go," Roscoe said.

Libby pushed his hand away as there was no way that she could go down several flights of stairs with a shirt over her face. "I'm fine."

Roscoe's blue eyes were wide with fear as they searched hers. Then he seemed to relax a bit, giving a slight nod. "Okay, let's get out of here."

She didn't really think a visit to the emergency department was necessary, but the thought of fentanyl powder on their clothing was enough to convince her to go along with the plan.

Rhy was on the phone as they took the stairs to the main level. She wasn't sure who he was speaking with, but it sounded like maybe his family. Likely the two women he'd mentioned that work there.

Apparently, Rhy came from a big family, very different from what she had experienced. Thinking of her brother's murder made her sad.

Had Tony been exposed to fentanyl in the same way they'd been? It was difficult to imagine how anyone could get highly potent drugs into the prison system. Not without help from a guard or two.

"This way." Rhy turned and headed down a long hallway.

She and Roscoe followed, all three of them taking care not to brush into anyone or even each other along the way. She didn't think her clothes had been contaminated, but Roscoe had wedged his large frame between her and the man who'd possessed the drugs.

A pretty woman with brown hair, wearing a long white lab coat and a cute maternity top met them outside the emergency department. "I'll need all three of you to head into the decontamination area. We have three sets of scrubs for you to change into."

"What does that mean?" Libby didn't understand. "You don't expect us to strip down to our underwear, do you?"

"Yes, exactly. You'll need to get rid of all of your clothing." The pretty doctor's eyes were sympathetic. "It's better to take precautions than to risk your life or that of your baby. The nurse waiting inside will take your purse and any electronics too. We'll have to wipe them down with disinfectant."

"Thanks, Faye," Rhy said. "Stay back here, though. I don't want you to be exposed."

"I'll be careful. Dana Callahan is waiting inside," Faye said.

Rhy and Roscoe waited for her to step forward, maybe because her clothes were the least likely to be contaminated. She told herself it didn't matter if she had to strip down in front of these two men. Rhy was married, and Roscoe—well, he'd already seen her, hadn't he?

Still, her cheeks burned as she stepped into a shower-stall-like area. A cute dark-haired nurse was standing beside a stack of supplies. "Put these gloves, goggles and mask on," Dana directed. "Then take your clothes off and leave them on the floor, including your shoes. Once you've done that, carefully remove your gloves first, then your face mask and goggles. From there, you'll go into the shower area. Roscoe and Rhy will wait here; I won't let them come in until you're finished, okay?"

"I understand." She followed Dana's directive, feeling slightly reassured that she would be alone in the shower. After donning the protective devices, she peeled off her maternity top, then did the same with her maternity capri pants, followed by her underclothes. Then she stepped away and carefully removed her gloves, goggles, and mask. Glancing over her shoulder, she was relieved to see Dana standing there without the two men.

"Great. Now step into the next room," Dana said. "You'll take a shower, getting your hair wet, too, in case there are particles of fentanyl there. When that's finished, you'll find towels in the next room, along with a clean pair of scrubs and hospital slipper socks for your feet."

"Okay. Here goes." It was a big room for a shower. After washing herself from head to toe, she stepped out of the shower and found the towels and scrubs as promised.

She was dressed and waiting in another room by the time Rhy and Roscoe had followed the same decontamination procedure.

"Dr. Finnegan, would you please make sure Libby gets examined by a doctor?" Roscoe asked once they were all together again, and Dana had brought them back to the emergency department. "I just want to be sure she and the baby are doing okay."

"Of course. This way." Faye Finnegan led them down a hallway to the back side of the emergency department. She found an empty room and gestured for Libby to go inside.

"Sit tight for a few minutes. I need to get Libby registered as a patient and assigned to a care team," Faye explained.

"I have more calls to make." Rhy lifted the phone in his hand. "Stay here with Libby, I'll be back in a few."

"Sure." Roscoe helped her get up onto the gurney, then dropped into the closest chair. "I feel better now that we've ditched our clothes."

"Yeah." Her hair was still wet, despite her attempt to dry it with a towel. Roscoe's hair was wet, too, and he looked pale and shaken. "How did you know that guy had drugs?"

"He was wearing thin hospital gloves, which was odd. Especially since he wasn't dressed in scrubs or a lab coat. As he pulled his hand from his pocket, I just knew." Roscoe slowly shook his head, looking dazed. "I hope the staff members closest to him will be all right."

"I hope so too." She sent up a silent prayer for each of them. They didn't deserve to die because someone had targeted her. Then she frowned. "How did that man know we'd be here in the hospital?"

"Another good question." Roscoe sighed. "I don't know for sure, but it's possible the cartel had someone lurking around in the hospital, waiting to see who showed up to talk to Gonzales."

She frowned. "That man had a visitor tag on, though, didn't he?"

"I think so." He put a hand to his scrub top, then dropped it again. Their visitor tags had been disposed of during the decontamination process. "That's probably part of what Rhy is working on. I hope the perp doesn't die either. We need to know who hired him."

First, Juan Gonzales's seizure, then a guy going down with the same drugs he'd tried to use against them. Whoever was responsible for hiring these men was not fooling around.

"You still think Charlie Olson is responsible," she murmured.

"Yeah. Must be someone with access to information and the ability to find guys willing to do the dirty work." Roscoe straightened as a beautiful blonde nurse entered the room.

"Hi, I'm Alanna Carmichael. I understand you were exposed to toxic chemicals."

"Most likely fentanyl," Roscoe said grimly. "Based on the way two staff members and the perp himself went down."

"I heard all about it from my brother." Alanna eyed them with concern. "I'm sure the testing will come back soon." She turned toward Libby. "How are you feeling?"

"Okay. Maybe a little tired." She waved a hand. "I don't think I was exposed to the drug, though, thanks to Roscoe's quick thinking."

"I'm sure you're right, but I'm going to listen to your heart and lungs and to the baby's heartbeat too." Alanna took the stethoscope from around her neck.

Libby sat back, breathing slow and steady as Alanna examined her. She used the stethoscope on her belly, too, a smile curving her features.

"Everything sounds good," Alanna said. "We have an OB doc coming down to take a look, too, just to be extra cautious."

"Thank you." Libby was touched by the care and consideration they were giving her. The brief wooziness she'd felt earlier, was gone now. And she wasn't even sure that was from the brief drug exposure or her imagination.

Five minutes passed before a kindly balding OB physician entered the room, pulling an ultrasound machine along with him. "Good afternoon, I'm Dr. Martin. You're Libby Hall?" He glanced at Roscoe. "And you're the baby's father?"

"Yes," she and Roscoe said at the same time.

Dr. Martin laughed. "Okay, I'm going to do a quick ultrasound to check on your baby." He pulled the machine close to her bed. "Dad, you'll want to come over here to watch."

Roscoe jumped to his feet and went to the other side of the bed. When he took her hand, she held it tight.

"Cold gel," Dr. Martin said, lifting her gown while making sure the blanket covered her lower body. He flipped on the machine and then pushed the tip of the probe into the gel, working around her abdomen. After a few seconds, the quick beat of their baby's heart filled the room.

"That's amazing," Roscoe murmured, his gaze focused on the screen. "I can see the baby right there."

"Yes, and your baby's heart sounds nice and strong," Dr. Martin said with a nod. He moved the probe a bit more. "This is the baby's face."

"Beautiful," she whispered, unable to tear her gaze from the image. The baby had been moving and kicking for weeks now, but seeing the baby's face in her womb was mesmerizing.

"I agree, he or she is absolutely beautiful," Roscoe murmured.

"Sorry, the baby is too big to get a good view of the gender," Dr. Martin said with regret. He clicked a few buttons, and a small picture emerged from the machine. "It will be a nice surprise on delivery. For now, I'm satisfied the baby is doing fine."

"Thank you, Doctor," Libby said, her voice barely a whisper. She wanted to protest when Dr. Martin removed the probe from her belly and shut down the ultrasound. Then he handed them the picture he'd taken of their baby's face.

She glanced up at Roscoe. He surprised her by leaning down to kiss her.

"Beautiful," he murmured again. And this time, she didn't think he was talking about their baby.

Not the way his gaze bored into hers.

I LOVE YOU.

While Roscoe didn't say the words out loud, he knew them to be true. Too bad Libby wasn't ready to hear them.

And the timing was lousy. They'd barely escaped being drugged by fentanyl in the middle of the hospital. A place that should have been safe and secure.

"Dr. Martin said you're ready to be discharged," Alanna said, entering the room. Her eyes widening a bit, as if realizing what she'd interrupted. "Sorry, but we've been busy, and I really need to get you out of here, so we can bring other patients in."

"Not a problem," Libby said, her voice breathless. "What about these scrubs?" She gestured to the outfits they were still wearing.

"Take them with you." Alanna waved a hand dismissively. "Give them to Rhy when you're finished, and he'll get them back to me."

"Guess we'll need to stop at a store to replace our

clothes," Roscoe said, hoping there would be an easy way to do that while keeping Libby safe.

"No need, you'll both come to my house." Rhy entered the hospital room. "I have things that should fit you Roscoe, and my wife, Devon, has maternity clothes for Libby." He glanced ruefully down at his scrubs. "This isn't the first time I've had to borrow hospital scrubs."

"And probably not the last." Alanna patted her brother's arm consolingly. "Glad you're okay, too, Rhy."

"Yeah, thanks to Roscoe." Rhy turned toward Libby. "I'm not sure if we have shoes that will fit. Elly may have left a few pairs of flip-flops behind."

"We'll make do." Roscoe helped Libby slide off the cart, making sure her gown was securely fastened in the back. "Thanks for the offer, boss."

"It's the least I can do. I didn't have a good view of the guy to know he had drugs. Your quick actions saved all our lives." Rhy led the way through the emergency department like a man who'd spent a lot of time there. As they stepped into the hallway, he slowed, waiting for them to catch up. "Sadly, the staff members who were exposed are in critical condition."

The news made him wince. "How bad?"

"Not sure. They were given Narcan right away, but the young woman closest to the perp had a significant expo-sure." He hesitated, glancing at Libby, then added, "The perp is dead. Not only did he get the full dose of the poison he brought in, but he didn't get Narcan as quickly as the two staff members did."

Roscoe knew he should feel bad for the guy, but he didn't. "The worst part of that outcome is we'll never know who hired him."

"I have our team members working on finding his identity," Rhy said. "Don't give up hope yet. If he has a phone or any other device, we may be able to get a line on the person who hired him."

That was encouraging. Yet knowing the two staff members were fighting for their lives was far more depressing. He sent up a silent prayer for God to heal them as he took Libby's hand and continued down the long hallway.

People stared at them curiously as they headed back to the parking garage. It felt strange to walk around with nothing but slippers on his feet.

Rhy paused by his car. "Meet you at the homestead." At his confused glance, he added, "My house in Brookland." Rhy rattled off the address, and Roscoe committed it to memory.

Roscoe had never been there but had heard from other members of the team that Rhy and his wife, Devon, lived in a large six-bedroom house where the Finnegans had grown up. There were nine Finnegan siblings, including a pair of twins, Alanna and Aiden, so six bedrooms wasn't as extravagant as it sounded.

"Why do they call it the homestead?" Libby asked, once they were settled in the SUV and following Rhy out of the parking garage.

"No clue." He glanced at her, then lifted a hand to pat the scrub pocket where he'd tucked the ultrasound picture. "Have you thought about names? For the baby, I mean."

"Not really." She shrugged, then added, "Another reason I should have learned the baby's gender."

He wanted to ask if he would have any input as to the baby's name but decided he shouldn't push it. Seeing the baby's face and hearing the quick and steady heartbeat had been an amazing experience. He didn't have the right to ask for more.

Whatever name she wanted would be fine with him.

The drive from the hospital to Brookland didn't take long. The Finnegan homestead was a large redbrick dwelling with white trim and black shutters. Roscoe parked behind Rhy in front of a spacious three-car garage.

"Very nice," Roscoe said.

"Thanks." Rhy glanced at the house, then shrugged. "Sometimes I forget how blessed we are. It was touch-and-go during those early years after our parents died. I wasn't sure we'd be able to keep the place, but we managed."

"It's lovely," Libby chimed in.

"Follow me." Rhy stepped through the garage, reached up to key in an alarm code, then held the door open for them. He followed Libby inside.

"Hello, I'm Devon, and this is Colleen." A pretty woman with dark hair and blue eyes held a chubby baby roughly eight months old in her arms as she greeted them warmly. "Rhy called to let me know you needed to borrow a few things."

"We appreciate your help," Roscoe said. "I'm Roscoe Turner, and this is Libby Hall."

"Nice to meet you," Libby murmured. "Are you sure you don't mind lending me your maternity clothes?"

"Of course I don't mind." Devon smiled as Rhy crossed over to kiss her and then did the same with the baby. "I won't need them for a few months yet. I'm only eight weeks along."

"Colleen will have a brother or sister early next year," Rhy said with a grin.

Roscoe had heard the rumor of Rhy and Devon expecting, but it sounded like it was official. "Congrats."

"And congrats to you too," Devon said, smiling at Libby. "When are you due?"

"Oh, not until early October." Libby blushed and glanced at him. "Hopefully, the danger will be over by then."

"I'll pray for both of you," Devon said. "Now come with me and we'll find something for you to change into."

Roscoe lingered in the kitchen with Rhy as Libby disappeared with Devon and Colleen. "Thanks for doing this, but I hope our being here isn't putting your family in danger."

"I appreciate that, but this won't take long." Rhy eyed him critically. "I think my clothes should fit well enough. We'll wait until the women are finished, then head up."

"Thanks." Roscoe didn't really care what he wore. The only issue would be having decent shoes to wear. His main focus was keeping Libby safe. "I don't like how we were found at the hospital. It feels like these guys have eyes everywhere."

"I agree." Rhy pulled out his phone. "Let me check on the status of our safe house."

He listened as Rhy connected with Joe. When his boss grimaced, Roscoe figured the news wasn't good. "Okay, thanks."

"It's still in use," Roscoe said.

"Yes, but it sounds like the place will open in a day or two at the most." Rhy sighed. "As soon as the current residents are gone, you and Libby can use it."

A day or two wasn't bad, yet Roscoe still felt far too vulnerable. The near miss at the hospital, especially after not getting any good intel from Juan Gonzales, had rattled him.

If he hadn't noticed the perp's gloved hands, he and Libby would be the ones fighting for their lives.

Or worse, dead.

"We really need to know who that guy is," Roscoe said, more to himself than to Rhy. "Maybe we can track his movements here in the city. Figure out when and where he got into town."

"We've been trying to do the same with Juan Gonzales but have come up empty-handed," Rhy said. "We have not been able to trace his name to any credit cards, rental cars, or any other paper trail."

"Cash only, huh?" Roscoe shouldn't have been surprised. Then he frowned. "I thought Juan Gonzales's car was recovered from near the City Central Hotel."

"We have the vehicle, but the VIN doesn't match the plates," Rhy admitted. "Gabe Melrose is still digging for information. Last I heard, the license plate belongs to a car in Oklahoma."

"Great." Roscoe sighed. "That means Gonzales swapped license plates between Texas and Milwaukee."

"That's the working theory." Rhy turned when Devon, Colleen, and Libby came down the sweeping staircase from the second floor. "Looks like it's our turn."

Roscoe nodded, his gaze tracking Libby. She looked adorable in a pink maternity top with white capri slacks. Her hair had been brushed and blow dried. She also wore a pair of sneakers on her feet.

"Everything fits," she said with a smile. "Devon is a lifesaver."

"I'm happy to help." Devon bounced Colleen on her hip. "Please keep them. I have more than enough."

Somehow, Roscoe managed not to pull Libby into his arms for a kiss. He skirted around the women to follow Rhy upstairs. Their search for clothes didn't take long. Less than five minutes later, he was back in the kitchen, wearing Rhy's jeans, T-shirt, and running shoes that were only slightly too big for him.

"We need to get out of here," he said in a low voice to Libby. "I don't want to put Rhy's family at risk. Better for us to head back to the motel."

"Okay." Libby's gaze lingered on Colleen as she crawled around on the floor. He couldn't help but wonder what she was thinking, but then she abruptly turned away. "I'm ready."

"Rhy? We're heading out." Roscoe noticed Rhy was staring down at his phone. "Something wrong?"

"We have an ID on our dead guy with the fentanyl," Rhy said. "His name is Alberto Morales. Does that sound familiar?"

"Not to me." He glanced questioning at Libby. "You?"

"No." Libby frowned. "Any updates on the staff members?"

"Still hanging in there, but the man who was farthest away is waking up." Rhy scowled. "We're waiting for the test results to know if the substance was fentanyl or some other opioid, but it sounds like the Narcan worked."

"Please keep me up to date with what you learn," Roscoe said. "We really need some sort of evidence to tie this all back to Charlie Olson."

"I will." Rhy walked with them out through the garage and to the car. "Stay safe."

"That's the plan." He opened the door for Libby, then ran around to get behind the wheel. "Don't forget to call me with news."

"I won't." Rhy stood in the driveway as he backed out and headed toward the interstate.

"They're such a nice family," Libby said.

He nodded, keeping an eye on the rearview mirror as he

drove. "I like working for Rhy and Joe. They're the best bosses I've ever had."

"I can understand why," Libby said, her tone wistful. "Rhy leads by example."

"True." He noticed a badly dented and rusted silver Chevy truck keeping pace behind him. It seemed odd to have picked up a tail after leaving Rhy's house, and really strange to use a vehicle that stood out from a mile away, but he kept a wary eye on the truck as he changed lanes.

The dented and rusted truck changed lanes too. He slowed his speed; the truck did the same.

No way. This couldn't be happening again.

"What is it?" Libby twisted in her seat to look behind them.

"Hang on." Up ahead, Roscoe could see a break in the median between the two sides of the three-lane interstate. He knew that was a prime location for state patrol officers to sit and catch speeders.

He moved into the left lane, then abruptly hit the brake and wrenched the wheel to the left, turning into the narrow opening. Car horns blared, followed by the distinct sound of gunfire.

"Stay down!" He drove along the shoulder until he could merge into traffic heading in the opposite direction. Then he hit the gas, speeding past the other cars as fast as he dared, while praying they'd lost the truck for good.

CHAPTER NINE

Bending over in the passenger seat wasn't easy while six months pregnant. Libby tried her best to slide down to keep her head low as gunfire rang out.

Her body rocked sideways when Roscoe abruptly turned to the left in the middle of the freeway.

For long moments, there was nothing but silence. When she realized she was holding her breath, she let it out in a heavy sigh.

"How?" The word was a croak. "How did they find us?"

"I don't know." Roscoe smacked the steering wheel with the palm of his hand, betraying his frustration. "We don't have any of our clothes or our own phones. The vehicle should be clean."

Should be, but maybe wasn't. He didn't have to say the words for the thought to flash in her mind.

"Maybe there are more cartel guys hanging around in the area than we realized." She inched her head up, noticing they were heading back toward the lakefront. The completely wrong direction from where their motel was located. "They could have had one of them watching the hospital from the street."

"And that guy managed to pick us out of a crowd?" Doubt laced his tone. He dug for his phone, then used his thumb to dial a number. "Rhy? We took gunfire from a rusty and dented silver Chevy truck."

She couldn't hear Rhy's response but could imagine the news wasn't welcome. Rhy had a family to protect. His wife was pregnant, and they had a young daughter.

"I'm heading east," Roscoe said. "But I need a new vehicle. I don't understand how these guys are tracking us."

Again there was a brief silence as Rhy responded. Then Roscoe glanced over his shoulder and eased into the right lane. She wasn't surprised when he took the next exit.

"Okay, meet you at the precinct." With that, he dropped the phone into the cupholder. "I'm super frustrated by this."

She had to admit ducking from gunfire was getting old. "Does Rhy have any theories as to how the cartel keeps finding us?"

"The only logical explanation is that Charlie Olson has better resources than we anticipated." He scowled. "Maybe even MPD resources. It's possible the cop watching over Juan Gonzales is involved."

His comment sounded a bit paranoid, yet she had to admit these bad guys kept popping up out of nowhere. And someone had tried to kill them in the middle of the hospital with fentanyl.

Maybe the police officer standing guard at Juan Gonzales's bedside was a part of this.

She didn't say anything as Roscoe made his way to the precinct. *My second time in a police station*, she thought as he drove around to the back of the building.

"Stay close." He scanned the area as he slid his arm around her waist. He led her toward a nondescript door. Moments later, they were safe inside the precinct.

"Do you know all the officers who work here?" she asked in a hushed voice.

"Not personally, but I know of them." He kept his tone low too. "We're not going to talk to anyone outside of my tactical teammates."

That was fine with her. She had no idea who they could trust outside those closest to him. He led the way to the office area.

"Hey, Roscoe. Libby." Joe greeted them with a somber expression. "I heard you picked up a tail shortly after leaving the Finnegan homestead."

"Yeah. And that was after Alberto Morales tried to kill us with fentanyl at the hospital." Roscoe closed the office door behind them. "What do we know about that officer who stood guard over Juan Gonzales?"

"Rhy told me to check into him. His name is John Pollack." Joe glanced at a note on his desk. "Been with the department for about a year, transferred here from Houston, Texas."

Texas? Her eyes widened in shock. What were the chances of that?

"Why did he come here?" Roscoe demanded.

Joe hiked a brow. "Why did you?"

Roscoe glanced at her and flushed. "I told you the story about how I helped bring down a drug trafficker and decided to relocate to Milwaukee to live with my cousin Cameron Stevenson. That's totally legit. But hearing the cop guarding our cartel member is also from Texas is a big red flag."

"Maybe, maybe not." Joe shrugged. "Pollack claims he followed his girlfriend here. They met in college, and she got a job in a big name accounting firm here in Milwaukee."

"We need to follow up on his story," Roscoe said with a dark frown. "I don't believe in coincidences."

"I don't like them either," Joe shot back. "Or danger from out of state showing up on our doorstep."

Roscoe paled as if he'd been slapped. She put a hand on his arm as if that would prevent him from lashing back.

"Technically, I'm the one who brought danger to your doorstep," she said firmly. "I was threatened back in Rio Grande City and then was followed here. Two guys in a truck shot at me several times. This isn't Roscoe's fault."

"I know, I didn't mean to insinuate that it was." Joe grimaced. "Sorry. I'm on edge too. I was just pointing out that it works both ways. It's difficult to know who we can trust."

"I told Libby the only people I can trust are you, Rhy, and everyone on our tactical team," Roscoe said in a low voice. "No one else."

Joe nodded. "Everyone on the team trusts you, too, Roscoe. Especially me. You could be right about John Pollack. It's interesting that he came from Houston, although it doesn't seem likely that the cartel would plant him here a year ahead of time on the off chance that Libby would come to find you. The timing doesn't work to be linked to this."

Hearing Joe state it like that, she was forced to agree.

"But I'll see what we can find," Joe continued. "If he's dirty, we need to arrest him."

"Good." Roscoe looked slightly mollified. "Rhy mentioned using one of the undercover vehicles. What about the new Jeep?"

"It's yours." Joe tossed him the key fob. "Try not to get it shot up, though. Assistant Chief Michaels is leaning on Rhy to cut costs."

"If the Jeep gets shot up, it won't be our fault," Libby felt compelled to point out. "We've been trying to stay off-grid."

"And we were safe until I was stupid enough to bring Libby to the hospital to talk to Juan Gonzales," Roscoe said sourly as he pocketed the key fob. "It's a miracle we weren't killed by that fentanyl exposure. Once we get back to the motel, we're not leaving until the safe house is available."

"That's understandable," Joe agreed. "Gabe Melrose has been working on tracking the names of these perps, which isn't easy since we're not sure if they're real or aliases. He's been glued to his computer for all day."

"How long are you going to let him work?" Roscoe asked. "It's quarter past three in the afternoon. Gabe usually shuts down at five."

"I've asked Rhy to approve some overtime for him." Joe sighed. "All the more reason not to damage the undercover Jeep."

"We'll do our best," she said, feeling defensive.

"I know you will." Joe offered a slight smile. "Look, we are all committed to protecting you and your baby. And we're just as frustrated as you are at how the bad guys keep finding you."

"Okay. Thanks." She was glad to hear they were all on the same team.

Roscoe turned toward the door, then stopped to glance back at Joe. "Have you been filling Doug Bridges in on these attempts against us?"

"Yeah. That reminds me, I almost forgot to tell you the latest." Joe rubbed the back of his neck. "Things are happening fast; Bridges was very concerned about the fentanyl exposure at Trinity Medical Center. He also wanted me to let you know that Charlie Olson has cut off all contact with the DEA."

She stared at Joe. "What does that mean?"

It was Roscoe who answered, his gaze narrowed with anger. "It means Charlie Olson has gone rogue."

THERE WAS no doubt in his mind that Olson was the leak. Or one of them. Roscoe knew there could be several others tangled up in this mess. Like John Pollack from Houston. "I'm sure Olson is in Milwaukee by now."

"That's what Bridges believes," Joe said with a nod. "He is working with Olson's boss, Craig Wilke, but they haven't been able to get a line on Olson's location. Turns out, the DEA agent left his agency phone behind, sitting in the middle of the kitchen table in his home."

Roscoe frowned. "That's odd. Why not ditch it along the way?"

"Olson's boss thinks the cartel took him away at gunpoint, and he left his phone behind as a message to indicate he wasn't leaving willingly." Joe shrugged. "Bridges thinks he left it behind on purpose, as if to let everyone know he's no longer with the DEA. That after he takes care of business, eliminating the two of you, he'll be on a beach somewhere millions of dollars richer."

"I'm with Bridges on this," Roscoe said grimly. "Olson is dirty and doesn't care if we know it or not. He's pulling the strings of cartel puppets."

"You think a lot like Bridges," Joe said.

That may be true, but Roscoe wasn't ready to meet with the Milwaukee DEA agent in person again.

Not yet.

"Gabe should cross-reference Charlie Olson with John Pollack," he said. "Maybe there's a connection." As soon as he said the words, he realized that he was also linked to Olson. If not for Charlie Olson, he wouldn't have been in Rio Grande City in the first place to find the drugs at Tony's place. Which was exactly the point Joe had been trying to make earlier. "I know Olson asked me to find intel on Libby's brother, Tony Hall," he added hastily. "Makes me think Olson may have done the same thing with Pollack, hiring him to work some sort of angle as well. For all we know, Olson has been working with the cartel for years."

"That goes back to my theory," Libby said. "Olson must be working for a cartel that is upset that other cartels are infringing on their turf. That's why he asked you to find and arrest Tony."

"I agree with you, but it could also be as simple as Olson needing to make some arrests in order to justify himself as a DEA agent." Roscoe wasn't sure what the bigger picture was because a big chunk was missing. "We need more information."

"We're on it," Joe said. "Gabe is doing his best with all the intel we've tossed at him. Your job is to keep Libby safe."

He nodded slowly. Keeping Libby safe was all that mattered, yet he didn't like sitting on the bench while others jumped into the game. "Please call when you have something."

"Of course." Joe stepped forward to clap him on the back. "Take care, Roscoe. You too, Libby."

Libby inclined her head without saying anything.

Roscoe sensed she was still upset with Joe, and the way she jumped to defend him was sweet.

He followed her out of Joe's office and back to the rear exit to the precinct parking lot. As it was approaching change of shift, there were dozens of officers milling about, getting ready for roll call.

It wasn't easy to look at his fellow brothers and sisters in blue without suspicion. He avoided direct eye contact as he opened the side door for Libby, then followed her outside. The warm summer sun beat down upon their heads, but his heart was chilled.

Charlie Olson was out there. Looking for them. Waiting for them.

The replacement Jeep was parked in the far corner of the parking lot. He unlocked the car as they walked.

"Are we going back to the Red Mill Motel?" Libby asked as he opened the passenger door for her. A wave of heat hit hard; the interior was like an oven.

"Yes. Stay here, give me a minute to crank the air." He slid in behind the wheel and pushed the start button. The motor jumped to life. He turned the air-conditioning on high, waiting for the air to become cool enough to combat the heat.

Five minutes later, they were back on the road. He kept a wary eye on the rearview mirror, half expecting another truck to come roaring up behind them.

For once, he didn't see anything remotely suspicious.

Yet he wasn't going to be caught off guard again. He turned to head north, going out of his way to take a circular route back to the Red Mill Motel. Libby frowned at first but didn't say anything.

"You look upset," he said, breaking the prolonged

silence. "Joe is a good guy. He was only pointing out that we shouldn't jump to conclusions."

"I was upset with him at first, but it's fine." She rubbed her temple. "Don't mind me, I'm just tired."

"The baby?" He gave her a quick glance. "That OB doc seemed to think you and the baby were fine."

"We are." She yawned, then blinked. "I've often read about how people crash after experiencing an adrenaline rush but never really understood how it felt until now. One minute, my heart is racing, the next I want to crawl into a corner to take a nap."

He relaxed at that. Seeing the image of his baby's face on the ultrasound screen made him acutely aware of the danger. He'd managed to save the photo of their baby's face; it was tucked in his wallet. If something bad happened to Libby or their baby, he'd never forgive himself. "Take a nap," he said lightly. "I'll make sure we're not followed."

"I'll try." She rested her head against the window, then straightened. "You really think Charlie Olson is in the Milwaukee area?"

"Yes. I do." He glanced at her. "But try not to worry. Charlie hasn't been doing the dirty work himself. And we've managed to take out two of his cartel members so far."

"I keep wondering why he's decided to come after me now." Her brow furrowed. "Tony was in jail, and you were gone. What caused things to change?"

It was a really good question, and one he should have considered before now. "You're right. There must be a reason Charlie Olson jumped into action." A horrible thought hit. "He may have found out you were pregnant and knew you'd come to find me."

"But I didn't try to find you until someone broke into

my house and left a knife embedded in my kitchen table." She shook her head. "Before that, everything was fine."

"Yeah. But you made a point of visiting your brother in prison two weeks before all this happened." He reached over to take her hand. "What did Tony say? Did he deny being involved in drugs?"

"Yes, he tried to convince me he was innocent. But isn't that what all prisoners say? 'It wasn't me. I didn't do it.' Yeah, right." She scoffed. "I asked why he was working with the DEA if he wasn't guilty. He didn't have a good answer for that. Then I told him I personally saw the drugs in his house, so there was no point in lying to me. He looked shocked by that. And also surprised that I was pregnant," she added.

"Then what happened?"

She rolled her eyes. "He told me not to visit anymore. And then he left the visitation room." Her expression softened. "I wish I had known that it would be the last time I'd ever talk to him."

"I'm sorry. Whatever Tony did or didn't do, he didn't deserve to die." He gently squeezed her hand, although his thoughts were still whirling.

What if Tony was innocent? The drugs could have been planted in his house. Charlie Olson could have set Roscoe up to find them, springing the trap.

But why? What was the point of framing Tony Hall, then going after Libby? Was this really the work of rival cartels?

Or something else?

What was he missing?

"Do you think Tony was oblivious to the drugs he was bringing in from Mexico?" Libby asked. "What if he believed the deliveries were legit? That he had no idea what was being transported in those boxes?"

"It's possible," he said slowly. He was still trying to reconcile the possibility that Tony was set up to be arrested. Had that been done only to prove Olson was doing his job as a DEA agent, or was there another reason behind his actions?

And why contact the police department in San Antonio for help?

There were far too many questions without answers. Roscoe found himself praying Gabe Melrose would find something to help break the case open very soon.

Getting back to the Red Mill took twice as long as it should have, but at least he was convinced they hadn't been followed. Seeing the Pine Cone restaurant, he was going to head over, but he noticed Libby was resting with her eyes closed.

Five o'clock was too early for dinner anyway, so he continued to the motel. Libby blinked when he killed the engine.

"I can't believe I fell asleep." She yawned again. "Sorry about that."

"Don't apologize. You obviously need to rest." A flash of guilt hit hard. Rest had not been high on the agenda for the past twenty-four hours. "Let's get you inside. You can sleep until you're ready to eat."

"I'm always hungry these days," she complained, removing her seat belt and sliding out of the car. "Either tired or hungry."

"Take a nap," he encouraged. There was no point in her trying to look at more mug shots. They had several cartel names to work with, and so far, every one of them had been a dead end.

Literally or figuratively.

"Maybe I will." After making a quick stop in the bathroom, she crawled into bed. In thirty seconds, her breathing deepened, and her body relaxed. Just like that, she was out.

He watched her for a long time, trying to understand why pregnancy made her more beautiful.

And why he wanted so badly to kiss her.

Oddly, the near miss at the hospital came rushing back. If he hadn't noticed Alberto Morales wearing gloves and pulling something from his pocket, he and Libby would be in the hospital's critical care unit.

Or the morgue.

Chilling enough to be fired upon from a distance, the attempt to drug them face-to-face was nerve-racking. The cartel wasn't known for suicide-type missions, not like some terrorists or active shooters were.

Morales must have known there was a possibility he'd be poisoned by the drugs too. Yet he'd come toward them with the intent to toss pure fentanyl in their faces with blatant disregard for his own life.

It didn't make sense. He scrubbed his hands over his cheeks. He wasn't thinking as clearly as he'd like. Maybe he needed a nap.

With renewed resolve, he turned to the computer. He hadn't heard from Gabe Melrose, so he sent the team's tech expert an email, asking for an update.

Gabe didn't respond right away. He sighed, assuming the guy had already headed home for the day. If there was information to share, he felt certain Gabe would call or email.

Staring at the computer screen, he logged into the police database system. He didn't have Gabe Melrose's technical expertise, but he couldn't sit there twiddling his thumbs either.

The name Charlie/Charles Olson was too common of a name to find anything worthwhile. And DEA agents didn't put themselves out there on social media, especially not if they were leading a double life. He tried digging into the names of the cartel members but came up empty.

He decided to focus on John Pollack, the transplant from Houston, Texas. Most officers weren't on social media, but sometimes their friends or family were.

It was slow going, and frustrating to boot. When Libby softly began to cry, he bolted out of his seat, weapon in hand, searching for the threat.

Relaxing only a bit when he realized she was still asleep but having a bad dream.

Willing his pulse to return to normal, he holstered his weapon and crossed to the bed. "Libby, wake up. You're having a bad dream."

She lifted one arm over her face, as if shielding herself from a blow. What in the world?

He put his hands on her shoulders. "Libby! Wake up!"

She dropped her arm and opened her eyes, staring at him in confusion, before letting out a deep sigh. "Roscoe? What's wrong?"

"You were having a nightmare." Releasing her shoulders, he sat on the edge of the bed. "You don't remember?"

"I—someone was trying to kill me." She grimaced and pushed herself into a sitting position. "That's more reality than nightmare."

"I know. I'm sorry." He searched her gaze. "I'm here if you want to talk."

She lowered her gaze and covered her belly with her

hands. "I wish we could go far away from here, where I could have my baby in peace."

His heart twisted in his chest. She deserved that and more. Yet as much as he would have liked nothing more than to take her away from here, he couldn't. Staying off the grid for months until her due date wasn't realistic.

They'd barely managed to stay off-grid here in the small towns located well outside of the city. And that was with funding from his teammates.

"I do too." He tried to smile reassuringly. "Hopefully, Gabe and Doug Bridges will find Charlie Olson and his associates."

"Yeah." She dropped her gaze to her belly. Then to his horror, fat tears rolled down her cheeks.

"Don't cry. Please, Libby, don't cry!" He shifted to gather her into his arms. To his shock, she turned into his embrace, resting her head on his chest. He'd never felt more helpless in his life as her shoulders shook with sobs.

"Please . . ." He didn't know what to do or what to say. In truth, she had every right to be angry with him. With the situation they'd found themselves in.

After what seemed like an eternity, she stopped crying. She sniffled loudly and lifted her head. "I need a tissue."

He didn't want to leave her but rose to grab the small box of tissues from the bathroom. Handing it to her, he resumed his seat on the edge of the bed.

She blew her nose and wiped at her face. "Sorry about that. I could blame the hormones, but I'm pretty sure this is a delayed reaction from the fentanyl incident at the hospital along with being shot at after leaving Rhy and Devon's house."

"You don't have to apologize; I know how difficult it

must be for you." She surprised him by nestling close again. "I, uh, will do better in keeping you safe."

"Roscoe?" She lifted her head to look at him. "You're doing fine."

He wasn't, but before he could say anything, she kissed him.

At first, he wasn't sure she really meant to do this, but when her lips clung to his, he crushed her close, kissing her the way he'd wanted to the moment she'd arrived on his doorstep, pregnant and defiant.

Wishing with all his heart that this was a precursor to their future. Together.

As a family.

CHAPTER TEN

Kissing Roscoe was better than she had allowed herself to remember. Libby had wrestled with so many regrets about her relationship with him that she had been convinced he wasn't nearly as handsome as she'd thought.

She was wrong. He was more attractive than ever, especially while treating her with such kindness and compassion. She needed him well beyond keeping her and their baby safe.

He lifted his head and pressed a kiss to her temple. "That was amazing, but I don't want to take advantage of the situation," he murmured. "I know you didn't come here for this."

Hadn't she? Maybe not consciously, but deep down, she may have used the excuse of being in danger to rush to Roscoe's side. Outwardly, she'd been angry with him, hurt at how he'd used her.

But seeing him again had been wonderful. And kissing him was even better.

It was on the tip of her tongue to point out he hadn't

minded taking advantage of the situation over six months ago, but she managed to hold back.

No matter how much she wanted to pretend otherwise, they'd made that decision together. He hadn't taken advantage of her. If anything, it had been the other way around. Her shame and guilt had faded after she'd asked God for forgiveness.

Roscoe's phone rang. He instantly shifted away from her, rising to his feet to cross over to the desk to pick up the device. She missed his warmth.

"This is Roscoe," he said.

"Put the call on speaker," she whispered, wanting to hear the entire conversation.

"Hang on, Gabe. I'm putting you on speaker so Libby can hear this too." Roscoe lowered the phone and pushed a button. "Okay, go ahead."

She scrambled off the bed to join him, trying to smooth out the wrinkles in her clothes. Sleeping fully dressed normally wasn't comfortable, but she'd gone out like a light the moment her head hit the pillow.

"Okay, I found a connection between Pedro Alverez and the missing DEA agent, Charlie Olson," Gabe said. "Looks like Olson participated in arresting Alverez two years ago."

"Olson? I guess I assumed that was one of the local cops. We learned shortly after the arrest the evidence went missing, so Alverez was released from custody." Roscoe met her gaze. "Libby said she saw him outside her brother's apartment building. But how exactly did the evidence get tampered with?"

"I don't have a good answer for that one," Gabe said with regret. "Doug Bridges is working on digging into how the stuff disappeared. Now that Olson is in the wind, Bridges has issued a BOLO for Charlie Olson and Pedro Alverez. Oh, and Alverez is a legal US citizen from what I can tell."

"That's good work, Gabe," Roscoe said. "I hope both of them get picked up before they can cause any more harm."

"That's the goal," Gabe agreed. "I was able to get confirmation that the drug you and the hospital staff were exposed to was pure fentanyl."

She put a hand on her belly, feeling sick. Of course, that had been the working hypothesis, but to hear it stated so bluntly made her shiver.

"I'm glad you, Libby, and Rhy were able to escape relatively unharmed," Gabe went on. "That stuff is lethal."

"I'm glad we were able to walk away unscathed as well," Roscoe agreed. "Any updates on the hospital staff who were exposed?"

"They're still in critical condition, as is Juan Gonzales," Gabe said. "I wish I had more information, but that's all I have so far. These guys being illegal and working under aliases is making my job difficult."

Libby could tell Roscoe was disappointed. But he masked his feelings. "I appreciate everything you've gotten for us so far, Gabe. Good work."

"Thanks. I'm heading home, but I'll be back at it first thing in the morning," Gabe said. "Be careful out there, Roscoe. We have to assume that any one of these guys could be carrying more fentanyl."

"I hear you," Roscoe said, his features grim. "We'll be on high alert for that possibility."

"Thanks, Gabe." The thought of being exposed to fentanyl again made her stomach clench.

"Later." Gabe ended the call.

She dropped onto the edge of the bed, swallowing hard.

As if it wasn't bad enough to fear men with guns, now they had to worry about protecting themselves from fentanyl too. The decontamination process had been thorough, but what if the next time they were exposed outside the hospital? How soon would they be able to get the medical care they might need?

Too long.

"Are you okay?" Roscoe sat beside her, wrapping his arm around her waist. "You look pale."

"I'm fine." Her tone wasn't convincing either of them. "Maybe we should get gloves and face masks."

"That's a good idea." Roscoe hugged her for a moment, then stood. "We can stop at a store after dinner. Ready to hit the Pine Cone restaurant?"

"Sure." Maybe food would make her feel better. One thing about being pregnant was that her baby made his or her needs known with blatant disregard as to how she felt about it. If the baby needed protein, she had to eat whether she wanted to or not.

This was one of those times.

"Okay, let's go." Roscoe offered his hand. She allowed him to help her up and to lead the way outside. Glancing around, she noticed the Red Mill Motel was surprisingly busy. There were several cars in the parking lot alongside the newly borrowed Jeep.

"The Fourth of July holiday is coming up," Roscoe said as if reading her mind. "These people are likely enjoying a three-day weekend."

"I'm sure cops don't love that," she said as he opened the passenger door for her.

"Nope, long weekends only make our jobs harder." Roscoe shrugged. "The good news is that Gabe will keep working the case for us regardless of the upcoming holiday."

She nodded. Teaching wasn't easy, and the pay was lousy, but at least she had holidays and summers off. Yet without Roscoe's cop instincts and connections, she'd probably be dead. The differences in their jobs were like night and day.

Roscoe drove the short distance to the restaurant. Under normal circumstances, she'd have preferred to walk. While the summer sun was warm, it wasn't nearly as beastly hot as it was back home.

Inside the Pine Cone, there was a huge display case of what appeared to be home-baked goods. There were plenty of people standing in line and waiting for an order, but the restaurant itself had several empty tables.

"This way," the hostess said, grabbing two menus as she wove through the restaurant. Libby slid into the booth across from Roscoe, then gratefully accepted the proffered menu.

"I shouldn't be hungry," she muttered to herself as her mouth watered at some of the menu offerings. "I can't get over how much variety there is here."

"It's not all barbecued ribs, chicken, or tacos," Roscoe agreed. "Although I can't deny I like barbecued food."

"Exactly." She beamed. "I'd like the baked chicken and mashed potatoes with gravy."

"Don't forget the lemonade," Roscoe teased as their server approached with two glasses of water.

"Oh, I'm switching to milk. The last glass of lemonade gave me heartburn, and I like milk more now than I used to." That had been another pregnancy surprise. Some of her teacher colleagues had talked about having cravings for ice cream or pickles. She'd only craved milk.

After they placed their orders, she played with her straw. "I wish we knew how to find Olson and Alverez."

"The police will find them." He spoke with confidence, but she could tell he wasn't convinced. "They'll make a mistake soon enough."

Would they? It seemed to her that they'd already gotten away with killing innocent people.

It didn't seem right to be sitting here waiting for dinner while two innocent hospital staff members fought for their lives in the ICU after suffering a drug overdose that was meant for her.

"How do you do it?" She tossed her hands up in frustration. "I can't stop feeling guilty for being alive and well while others might die."

He reached across the table for her hand. "I don't know why we're alive while others are struggling. We could ask the same thing about many situations. I guess all we can do is accept our role in God's plan."

"That's easier said than done," she whispered.

"I know. We'll pray those staff members survive this." He bowed his head. "Dear Lord Jesus, please heal those who have been victims of this terrible crime. Amen."

"Amen." It didn't seem like enough, but she also couldn't come up with anything better. Was it wrong to want her baby to survive?

No, but she wished more than anything that those who wanted to kill her wouldn't hurt anyone else either.

When their meals arrived, she took another moment to thank God for their food. Roscoe bowed his head, too, then grinned at her.

It was strange the way they were in sync with each other. Was this why she'd lowered her guard when they'd first met?

Why she'd thrown caution to the wind to spend the night with him?

She still felt guilty for what she'd done, yet she couldn't regret having their baby.

This child was a blessing.

She had no idea what her future held, but the more time she spent with Roscoe, the more she knew he would not walk away from her and their baby.

The sooner she accepted his determination in helping her to raise their child, the better.

WHEN THEY'D FINISHED EATING, Roscoe paid the tab in cash, then asked their server where the closest drug store was located. Times like this, he missed having a smart phone.

The trip didn't take long, and soon they were back at the Red Mill Motel. He wasn't thrilled by the number of cars in the small parking lot, although they were somewhat helpful in hiding his Jeep.

He told himself to relax. Since they'd been back at the Red Mill Motel, he hadn't seen anything remotely suspicious. No tail, no one resembling a member of the Mexican drug cartel.

They were safe. For now.

After everything they'd been through since Libby had shown up on Cam's doorstep, he would have to be satisfied with that.

Libby still looked exhausted, despite her nap. She fell asleep while watching TV, while he wasted more time on the laptop, trying to think of a way to help find Charlie Olson or Alverez or anyone else who might be involved in this mess.

After hours of feeling useless, he gave up and crawled

into the second bed. He wanted to believe Gabe would uncover more information the following day.

He awoke when someone slammed a door nearby. With a wince, he glanced over to where Libby was still sleeping. Thankfully, she didn't stir.

Wishing for the comfort of the suite, he rolled out of bed and tiptoed to the bathroom. There was a small coffee pot in the room, with two packets of coffee, one regular and one decaf.

He held back from making a pot, not wanting to disturb Libby. The hour was barely seven in the morning. Gabe wouldn't be at his desk working until eight.

What in the world would he and Libby do all day? He couldn't bear the thought of sitting around doing nothing.

"I'm up." Libby's low husky voice interrupted his thoughts. "You've been staring at that coffee pot for a full minute. Go ahead and make some."

"After you're finished in the bathroom," he agreed.

Ten minutes later, he had made the decaf for her and was brewing a second pot of regular when his phone rang. He pounced on it, seeing Rhy's number on the screen and praying for good news.

"Rhy?" He quickly placed the call on speaker for Libby's sake. "What's going on?"

"Hey, Roscoe, Libby. I'm afraid I have bad news." Rhy sounded so dejected his stomach twisted. "Juan Gonzales died last night."

His first thought was that now they'd never know who had hired him, but then he remembered the guy had a son. The look of horror on Libby's face confirmed she had the same fear. "What about his son, Josue? Did Bridges find him?"

"Doug has received confirmation that a woman named

Maria Gonzales and her son, Josue Gonzales, crossed the border into Mexico two days ago," Rhy said. "Doug thinks that Juan insisted they head home to stay safe while he drove out here to Wisconsin. Doug is trying to contact them, both to ask a few questions and to notify them of Juan's death."

"That's terrible," Libby whispered.

"Don't forget how he shot at us through the door of our suite," Roscoe pointed out.

"He only did that because his son was threatened," Libby said defensively.

Roscoe wasn't sure Juan would have felt nearly as guilty as she did if he had succeeded in killing them. But he didn't say that. "I hope Bridges can talk to them. Maybe Maria knows something that will help."

"It's possible," Rhy agreed. "On a positive note, the two hospital staff members are still hanging in there. One has woken up and will be transferred to a regular room. The other is still unconscious."

"I'm glad," Roscoe said, meaning it. It was horrible how the staff members had been in the wrong place at the wrong time. Yet without them, he and Libby would have been the ones lying in hospital beds.

Rhy too.

"There's one more thing," Rhy said, interrupting his thoughts. "The DEA has been using the traffic cameras to find video of either Charlie Olson or Pedro Alverez. Do you have your laptop booted up? I'm sending you a grainy picture of a man who we believe is Charlie Olson, spotted on a camera not far from our precinct here in Milwaukee."

His chest tightened as he reached over to open the laptop. "I'm logging in now."

"Okay. We need you and Libby to take a good look at

this guy. Especially you, Roscoe. You've seen him in person. All we have is an old photograph from his DEA ID badge."

Libby hovered close to his side as he waited for his email to pop up. He double clicked on the attachment. The photo wasn't great, barely a profile view, but that was enough.

"Yeah, that's Olson." He glanced at Libby, then added, "I guess we know why he dropped off the radar."

"We'll find him," Rhy said. "Bridges asked Ian, the feds' tech guy, to play around with the photo until he could get the license plate number. The BOLO has been updated to include the make and model of the vehicle, along with the license plate. Granted, there are lots of black Kia SUVs out there. Oh, just so you know, the license plate is AG4822."

Roscoe made a note of it.

"With this information at hand, I'm convinced we'll find him," Rhy went on. "He can't hide forever."

"Okay, that's good." He felt slightly better knowing the feds were using their resources to complement what Gabe was doing. "I hope he stays in the city."

"We do too." There was a brief pause before Rhy said, "That's all I have for now. Just know we're working every angle possible."

"I want to help," he said. "There must be something we can do from here."

"I can check with Gabe, but your main job is to stay off the radar. Leave the investigating to us."

He didn't like that answer, and simply said, "Thanks, Rhy."

"Why do you think Charlie Olson took the risk to come all the way to Milwaukee?" Libby frowned. "You'd think he'd have gone to Mexico, or some other foreign country, to avoid being caught."

"I don't know, but don't worry. He's far away from our current location."

"I get that, but it still doesn't make sense. He must know the DEA has federal resources to track him down." She stood, stretching her back. "I don't like it. Seems too easy."

"I told you criminals often make mistakes." He shrugged, even though he secretly agreed with her. But he didn't want her to be stressed out and worrying about this. She had enough to be concerned about. "Olson strikes me as the type of guy to be arrogant enough to assume he won't get caught because he's better than everyone else."

"Maybe." She narrowed her gaze, as if sensing he was trying to shield her. "I'm hungry for breakfast. Is the Pine Cone our only option?"

"Afraid so." He took a sip of his coffee, grimacing at how it had already grown cold. "You enjoyed dinner last night, right? I'm sure they do an awesome breakfast too."

"Then what?" She threw her arms wide. "We sit here all day?"

He didn't like it any more than she did. "Yep. Let's hit the road."

"Can we at least walk?" She pushed her feet into the borrowed running shoes Devon had provided. "I sick of sitting."

After a brief hesitation, he nodded. "Sure. It's not far, barely a half mile."

"Great." She beamed as if he'd given her a priceless gift. "Thanks."

"Libby, when this is over, we really need to talk."

Her smile faded, and she looked away. "I know."

Her lack of enthusiasm was not reassuring. He led the way out of the motel room, sweeping his gaze over the parking lot before stepping forward so Libby could join him.

Walking to the Pine Cone didn't take long. He was glad no one seemed to pay them any attention as they headed down the street and over the bridge spanning the interstate to reach the restaurant. He supposed many motel guests took this same path.

Once they were seated at a booth on the opposite side of the restaurant this time and had given their orders, he tried to think of a way to approach the topic of how they would work together once the baby was born.

"After Olson has been arrested, I'll move back to Texas." He searched her gaze, then added, "I'll find a police department that's hiring."

She frowned. "I would never ask you to leave your position on the tactical team."

What did that mean? Was she interested in moving here? Their server returned to top off his coffee and to bring her a large glass of milk. He waited until they were alone again before leaning forward. "I don't care about my career as long as I'm close to you and our baby."

She sat back and folded her arms across her chest. "I thought we were going to discuss this once the danger was over."

"Just know I'll do whatever is necessary to make this work." He knew he was pushing, but he couldn't help it. "I plan to be a father to our child."

She averted her gaze, then shrugged. "We'll figure it out. It's hard to imagine what our life will be like when we have this threat of danger looming over us."

Maybe she was right to wait. He wanted more than to just be a father figure. He wanted it all.

But Libby wasn't ready for that. At least not yet.

She had kissed him, so all wasn't lost. Patience wasn't his strong suit, but he'd try to give her the time she needed.

When their breakfast arrived, she bowed her head. "Libby? I'd like to say grace."

Her head snapped up in surprise, but then she nodded. He held out his hand, grateful she took it.

"Lord Jesus, we ask You to bless this food and to continue keeping us safe in Your care. Amen."

"Amen." She held his hand for a long moment, before reaching for her fork. "Isn't this where you say dig in?"

He smiled and nodded. "Yep."

She took a bite of her veggie omelet and nodded. "It's good. Not as good as the chicken last night, but still tasty. It's strange not to be offered Tabasco sauce with your eggs."

"You'all aren't in Texas anymore," he drawled.

"I guess not." She dug into her breakfast with enthusiasm. "I don't know why I'm so hungry all the time."

He was about to remind her she was eating for two when his phone buzzed. Praying for news, he quickly answered Gabe's call. "Did you find him?"

"Not yet. Bridges really wants to talk to you. I know you've asked for information to flow through the team, but Rhy is tied up and the rest of the team is busy too."

He frowned, then realized he was probably being foolish. "Yeah, okay. But we're in a public place, so I'll have to call him when we're finished."

"That's fine. Let me give you his number." Gabe rattled off the digits, and he repeated them twice to make sure he'd committed them to memory.

"Got it." He glanced at his watch. "Tell him I'll call in about twenty minutes, once we're back at the motel."

"That works. Thanks, Roscoe." Gabe ended the call.

"Sounds like you no longer suspect Bridges of being

dirty." Libby eyed him thoughtfully, clearly having heard his side of the conversation.

"I don't. I'm convinced Charlie Olson is the mastermind behind this."

"I'm glad." She finished the last bite of her omelet and pushed her plate aside. "We need to trust someone within the federal government. I mean, your teammates are great, but Olson is a fed, or used to be. Federal agents like Doug have a better chance of tracking another federal agent." She frowned. "Or a former agent. I'm not sure if Olson has been officially fired or if he took time off."

"It sounds like he just didn't show up for work. Or tell his boss that he was working a case." His gaze narrowed. "I'm hoping he's on the way to being fired."

"Something you can ask Bridges when you call him back." She drained her glass of milk then stood. "I'll be back in a few minutes."

He nodded, digging in his pocket for cash to pay the tab. Despite the generous amount Jina and Zeke had given him, he felt like they were going through money faster than they should. When Libby finished in the restroom, he paid their server and headed outside.

Shielding his eyes from the sun, he took a moment to scan the Pine Cone parking lot.

There were plenty of cars; the restaurant did a brisk business for being so far outside the city. More than those staying at the Red Mill.

He took Libby's hand and walked along the side of the building toward the road. From here, he could see the entire parking lot of the Red Mill Motel.

A black SUV caught his gaze. He slowed, trying to get a better look, but they were too far to get a good look at the license plate.

Telling himself he was being paranoid, he turned to Libby. "Stay behind me, okay?"

"Why?" She sounded exasperated but released his hand and slowed her steps. They were almost to the bridge that spanned the interstate when he saw a man get out from behind the wheel of the black car.

No way. It couldn't be. But it was.

Charlie Olson had found them.

CHAPTER ELEVEN

"Get down." Roscoe's urgent tone had her dropping to her knees—no easy feat—looking around for a possible source of gunfire.

"What's happening?" She kept her voice low, trying to understand what had caught his attention. She didn't see anything alarming. And kneeling along the side of an overpass didn't seem smart. Granted, there wasn't a lot of traffic, but still, some people drove like maniacs.

"We're going back to the restaurant." Roscoe had placed his large frame in front of her. "You start; I'll cover you."

"Tell me what's going on." She rose with a muffled groan and turned to head back the way they'd come.

"Charlie Olson is at the Red Mill Motel." His tone was grim.

She glanced at him over her shoulder. He had looked back at the motel, too, before turning to face her. "Are you sure?"

"Oh yeah. Let's go." When they reached the edge of the embankment, Roscoe grabbed her arm. "Wait. Let's go down into the gully instead."

"Are you out of your mind?" She stared at him incredulously. "If I go down there, I'll never get back up!"

"We don't have a choice. Once Olson realizes we're not in our room, he'll come to the restaurant."

That made sense, but she didn't like it. Still, she began edging her way down the steep slope toward the cars racing back and forth on the interstate. Her heart hammered against her rib cage. One wrong move and she'd be down there, in the middle of harm's way.

As if reading her mind, Roscoe latched onto her hand. "Wait. Let me go first. I'll brace you."

She didn't want him to go rolling down onto the freeway below either and silently prayed he was strong enough to prevent them both from falling to certain death.

"Easy," he said, although the noise from the cars made it difficult to hear him. She was grateful for the running shoes Devon had loaned her, but the grass was still slippery. Twice she almost lost her footing, but Roscoe kept her upright.

After what seemed like eons, he nudged her toward a small corner of the embankment where there was a flat grassy area.

"Sit here." Roscoe put his mouth right by her ear so they could communicate. "You'll be shielded from view."

"What about you?" She gratefully and awkwardly lowered herself to the ground, fearing that getting back up would be a challenge.

"I'll be right here." He pulled out his disposable phone and worked the screen. She assumed he was texting someone from his team. Rhy, Joe, or one of the others as they needed a ride. Drawing a deep breath, she wished she hadn't insisted on walking to the Pine Cone. There was no way to sneak back to the motel to get the Jeep.

How long would it take Olson to get to the restaurant? And when Charlie didn't find them there, to begin searching the immediate area? He probably knew she was pregnant, so it wasn't like they could get far.

Roscoe would ask his teammates to come pick them up, but they'd purposefully gone well outside the city limits. By the time anyone from Milwaukee could get out there, it would likely be too late.

Pressing a hand to her chest, she tried to battle a wave of panic. Imagining every what-if scenario wasn't helpful.

Please, Lord Jesus, keep us safe in Your care!

"Libby?" Roscoe knelt beside her, leaning close so she could hear him. "I'm heading up to see if Olson is still at the motel."

A wave of fear had her grabbing his arm. "Don't leave me."

"I'm not going far." He pressed a kiss to her cheek. "I just need to know if he's still at the motel or if he's over at the restaurant."

"What if he finds us?" Their hiding spot wasn't exactly unique. Any idiot would figure out they had taken cover beneath the bridge.

"Doug and Zeke are on the way." He smiled reassuringly, then added, "I'm armed. If Charlie gets too close, I'll take him out."

His statement was far from reassuring. Charlie Olson was a federal agent, and they didn't have actual proof that he was involved in the attempts to kill them.

Of course, if Charlie fired at them first, then Roscoe would be justified in shooting back.

Before she could argue, Roscoe captured her mouth in a quick kiss. She clung to him for a moment, then released him. He quickly rose and made his way up the embankment. Within seconds, he had moved out of sight. The traffic was so noisy she couldn't hear him at all. A fact that might work to their advantage.

She prayed Doug and Zeke would get there in time to prevent gunfire and the inevitable bloodshed.

Not Roscoe's blood, please? She pulled her knees in as far as she could, trying to make herself as small as possible. As she watched the cars below zooming past, she was confident none of the drivers noticed her. No doubt they were keeping their eyes on the road rather than scanning the underpass for a person sitting beneath the shelter of the overpass.

In some ways, she liked feeling invisible. But she also knew this was a false sense of security. It was only a matter of time before Charlie Olson found them. It bothered her to know he'd shown up at their motel.

How many resources did he have at his disposal? The only way she could imagine they'd been found was by somehow tracking Roscoe's computer.

Movement caught the corner of her eye. Startling badly, she jerked around. Then relaxed when Roscoe appeared.

"Well?" She searched his gaze. "Is Charlie at the restaurant?"

"He's still at the motel, but I think he's getting ready to move." Roscoe bent closer so he could speak in her ear. "I need you to stay here no matter what happens. This is where Doug and Zeke will be looking for you."

"Please don't leave me." Begging wasn't her style, but the idea of Roscoe putting his life on the line by confronting Charlie Olson made her sick. "Stay close. He might not find us here."

"I'll be fine." He seemed immune to her plea, which spiked her temper.

"You're not a robot," she snapped. "You're flesh and blood, Roscoe. Charlie could easily kill you!"

"I have the element of surprise on my side." He glanced down at the traffic zipping by below. "Besides, I know Doug and Zeke will be here soon. They'll break speed records to get here in time."

"Not soon enough . . ." But it was no use. Roscoe was already turning to move back up the embankment, his weapon in hand.

Leaving her to little choice but to do nothing but wait.

And pray.

———

ROSCOE COULDN'T LET himself dwell on Libby's fear and anger. Since the moment she'd shown up on his doorstep, he'd known this time would come. He would gladly risk his life to protect hers.

Not just because she was pregnant; although, that was a factor. He would do the exact same thing if she wasn't.

Hopefully, Doug and Zeke would arrive in time.

He peeked up over the edge of the bridge, his heart sinking when he realized the black Kia SUV was gone. He turned and made his way to a better position to see the Pine Cone restaurant. There were still several cars in the lot, but no Kia from what he could see.

Olson may have parked along the far side or even around the back of the restaurant. That's what he would have done if their situation was reversed.

It would take at least five minutes for Olson to clear the restaurant. Maybe another two minutes for him to begin searching for them along the embankment.

This area was the only logical place for two pedestrians on foot to hide.

He flattened himself on the ground, keeping his gaze on the restaurant and patiently waiting for Olson to show himself. He could arrest the DEA agent for murder for hire, yet they were also well outside of Roscoe's jurisdiction.

Too bad. He'd take the risk. Besides, if Olson did anything remotely threatening, his plan was to shoot first and ask questions later.

No matter what happened, this guy would not hurt Libby.

A long, agonizing eight minutes later, Olson stepped out of the Pine Cone restaurant and looked around. It seemed as if Olson stared right at his hiding spot, but to his surprise, the DEA agent didn't reach for his weapon. Instead, the fed took one step forward and continued sweeping his gaze over the parking lot. Maybe he believed they were hiding in a vehicle nearby.

"Roscoe! I know you and Libby Hall are out there!"

There was no way on earth Roscoe planned to respond. Was this a lame attempt to pull him and Libby out of hiding? If so, the fed had underestimated him. Roscoe stayed down, aiming his weapon toward the center of Olson's chest. He was too far away for accuracy but would focus on hitting the guy's center mass.

"I know you're in danger," Olson continued. "I'm here to help!"

Yeah, sure. Roscoe wasn't fooled by the guy's attempt to come across as an ally. Just the opposite. He noticed Olson took a few steps forward as if intending to cross the parking lot. The way Olson glanced from side to side indicated the fed still didn't know exactly where they were hiding.

But it wouldn't be long before Olson zeroed in on his location.

"Come on, Roscoe. I'd like to help you hide from the cartel," Olson said. "There's a leak within the agency as I'm sure you've figured out already."

It was tempting to voice his belief that Olson was the leak, but Roscoe held his tongue and his position. The closer Olson came to his hiding spot, the better chance he had of taking the guy out of commission.

Olson's gaze continued to move back and forth, pausing for what seemed like a long second on Roscoe. The grass wasn't that long, so it wasn't a surprise that he'd been spotted. Before he could warn Olson off, he felt someone tug on his left foot.

Libby? *Please, Lord, not Libby!*

He didn't dare turn to glance behind him. His gaze never left Charlie Olson's approaching figure. It wouldn't be long until the fed reached the steep incline leading down to the interstate.

When he felt another hard tug on his foot, with enough force to pull him an inch down the embankment, he realized the person behind him couldn't be Libby. She couldn't lie on her stomach and was probably not strong enough to move his 180-pound frame.

Zeke and Doug had arrived.

He kicked out with his right foot in warning. Whoever was behind him didn't realize he had Charlie Olson in his sights.

The hand didn't release his foot, making him swallow a wave of impatience. Then he realized what Zeke or Doug intended. They probably wanted him to go down to a waiting vehicle.

Was there enough time to get out of there, without raising Charlie Olson's suspicions? He didn't know.

There was another tug on his foot. Clearly a message he couldn't ignore. He used his elbows to scoot backward, keeping his head down as much as possible. The continued and incessant tugging on his left ankle indicated that he was doing exactly what Zeke or Doug wanted.

It didn't seem right to leave Olson up there, but he went along with the plan. Once he was far enough away from the edge, he turned to see Zeke behind him. Zeke gave him an exasperated look as if silently asking what had taken him so long to get the message.

Beyond Zeke, he saw a black SUV parked at the side of the interstate. Even from here, he could see Libby sitting in the back seat.

"Get her out of here," Roscoe hissed. "Olson's up in the parking lot!"

"Doug and Brady Finnegan are going after him," Zeke said just as irritably. "Jina and I were tasked with getting you and Libby out of here."

It went against the grain to be treated like a victim instead of a cop. But since Doug had brought Brady along as backup, he relented. Now that Zeke wasn't pulling him, he allowed himself to slide the rest of the way down to the freeway, glancing over his shoulder twice to make sure Olson hadn't crested the top of the embankment. From there, it would be easy to shoot and kill him and Zeke both.

But there was no sign of him.

When they'd reached ground level, Zeke practically pushed him into the back seat beside Libby, then jumped into the passenger side. Jina hit the gas, picking up speed and watching for the moment she could ease into traffic.

"Are you sure Doug and Brady will get Olson?" Roscoe

asked. "I had him in sight. We could have held him in place until the two feds could get there."

"They were five minutes ahead of us," Jina said. "Doug's tech expert caught the vehicle on one of the traffic cameras."

"You really think they were already surrounding him at the Pine Cone restaurant?" He frowned. It was possible because he had only focused on Olson, not the possibility of someone coming up behind him.

"They're the feds," Zeke said with a shrug. "Our job was to get you and Libby out safely. Jina helped Libby get down, while I crawled up to get you."

"Thanks." He met Jina's arched look in the rearview mirror. He could tell she wasn't impressed with his ability to keep Libby safe. Although it wasn't his fault Charlie Olson had found them.

Unless it was? He swallowed hard. "Is it possible Olson tracked my computer to the motel?" He forced the question through his tight throat. "I logged into the police database, but that should have been a secure connection."

"We'd have to ask Gabe about that," Zeke said. "I'm not a tech expert, but I can't imagine how else he'd have been able to find you there."

"I had the same thought," Libby murmured. She reached for his hand, her gaze mirroring her relief.

"I never should have tried to work the case from the motel." He was annoyed with himself. Why couldn't he have just left it alone? He should have stayed focused on staying off-grid the way Rhy and Joe had recommended.

"I heard voices," Zeke said after a long silence.

"Yeah, he was trying to draw me out." Roscoe repeated what Charlie Olson had said. "I don't believe for one hot second that he wanted to keep us safe from the cartel. It was nothing more than a lame attempt to gain our trust."

"Doug and Brady will grab him." Jina spoke with confidence. "Rhy will let us know when that happens."

"Where are we going in the meantime?" Roscoe asked. "At some point, we'll need to pick up the undercover Jeep from the Red Mill."

"Rhy sent Grayson and Flynn to do that." Zeke turned and flashed him a grin. "Rhy promised Assistant Chief Michaels that he wouldn't go over budget this year. I think he was worried about getting that Jeep back intact."

He managed a smile. "I can understand his concern. Especially with as much overtime as Gabe has been putting in for us."

"I can't believe Charlie tried to get us to come out of hiding," Libby said with a scowl. "He must think we're stupid."

He gently squeezed her hand. "Olson doesn't realize how much technical and physical support we have from the tactical team." He gestured toward Zeke and Jina with his free hand. "He doesn't understand how we would go to the wall for each other."

"Yeah, the closeness we share is not normal in other police precincts," Jina said. "Trust me, I've seen other cops throw each other under the bus without an ounce of remorse."

It was the first time Jina had alluded to her past, which they all suspected was rife with secrets.

"You got that right," Zeke agreed. "And as far as your question goes, we have a room at the Timberland Falls Suites reserved for you."

"Timberland Falls, huh?" Roscoe sighed, remembering

last month when Grayson and Eve had used the place to hide out, only to be found by a shooter. "The cops there don't like us much."

"Yeah, I know." Zeke shrugged. "They'll get over it. Besides, once Doug and Brady get Olson into custody, the danger will be over."

"What if Olson doesn't call off the cartel members who are still looking for us?" Libby asked. "They won't know he's arrested."

"That's why we have the suite reserved," Jina admitted. "Besides, the cartel doesn't have the same type of resources the federal government has at its disposal. They won't be able to track you and Roscoe here without inside help."

"I guess that's true." Libby visibly relaxed in her seat. "I'll be relieved when this is over."

He nodded, even though deep down, he couldn't relax. He knew Jina was right about the cartels lack of resources. After all, it was Charlie Olson himself who had shown up at the Red Mill Motel, not his hired guns.

Now that he thought about it, he realized it was strange that Olson had been alone. He would have expected the fed to have cartel backup nearby.

Then again, Olson may have thought being alone would encourage them to come out of hiding.

Either way, he had no intention of relaxing his guard. Not until they'd heard from Doug and Brady that Olson was in custody and no longer a threat.

"Where is Timberland Falls?" Libby asked, breaking into his thoughts.

"It's a suburb a few miles outside of Milwaukee." He strove to sound reassuring. "Far enough away to be safe, yet closer to having backup as needed."

"I can't believe you and Zeke got to the overpass so fast," Libby said to Jina. "It took us forever to get to that motel."

"We used our red flashing lights." Jina flashed a cheeky grin. Roscoe didn't think he'd ever seen Jina smile so much as she had with Libby. "Cars moved over giving us plenty of room to top ninety miles per hour."

"Those vehicles knew you'd hit them if they didn't move," Zeke said, shaking his head. "I lost ten years off my life when you zipped around the two cars that didn't move fast enough."

"You're fine." Jina waved a hand. "Quit whining."

The trip to Timberland Falls took longer since they were not using red lights to bust through traffic. It bothered Roscoe that they hadn't heard from Rhy, and he found himself praying that Doug and Brady had gotten Olson into custody.

Surely two experienced federal agents wouldn't have let him slip away?

No, he couldn't go there. He needed to have faith. Knowing Rhy's expertise as a tactical officer, he knew his brother Brady would be equally good at his job.

"Finally," Roscoe muttered when the Timberland Falls Suites came into view. "Once we get inside, we should call Rhy."

"Boss promised to keep us in the loop," Zeke said with a shrug. "Give him some time. He probably doesn't have anything to give us yet."

He bit back a sharp reply, understanding his own impatience was getting to him. Zeke was right. Doug and Brady had to transport Olson to the federal office building before they could interview him on record.

And that was only if Olson cooperated. He figured the fed would be smart enough to ask for a lawyer, which would only delay things further. They would be lucky to get any pertinent information out of the guy by the end of the day.

He relaxed his tense muscles. Time to focus on the most important thing, that he and Libby were safe. Charlie Olson was far away and no longer a threat.

When Jina parked near the front lobby, he pushed out of the back seat. He went around to help Libby, but Jina beat him to it. He gave his teammate an exasperated glance, which she ignored.

Clearly, Jina hadn't forgiven him for leaving Libby behind in Texas.

Zeke led the way inside. Their suite was on the ground level, which suited Roscoe just fine. Better to be prepared in case he and Libby were forced to make another daring escape out a window.

"This is nice," Libby said, gazing around with admiration. "With all the talk of budgets, I'm surprised we're here."

"We've used this before, so there's no reason to worry about Rhy's budget." Roscoe glanced at Zeke. "Any chance Grayson and Flynn are bringing the undercover Jeep here?"

"I'll call them." Zeke pulled out his phone and walked to a far corner of the room. Roscoe noticed Libby had disappeared into one of the bedrooms with Jina. He hoped Jina wasn't convincing Libby to dump him.

A few seconds later, Jina returned. At his questioning look, she shrugged. "She wanted to use the bathroom."

"Oh." He was an idiot for not thinking of that. "She mentioned the baby likes to jump on her bladder."

Jina crossed the room straight toward him and jabbed her finger into his chest. "You better treat her right, Roscoe."

"I will." He held Jina's gaze. "I love her, Jina. But she needs time."

"Yeah, maybe." Jina dropped her hand and stepped back. "In some ways, she reminds me of my younger sister."

"You have a sister?" For some reason, the news shocked him.

Jina scowled and looked away without responding.

"I have Grayson and Flynn bringing the Jeep here," Zeke said. "Joe agreed, mainly because we could be called away in an emergency."

"Thanks." Roscoe was relieved. He didn't want to be stuck out here without a vehicle. Having to hide beneath the underpass was bad enough. Libby wouldn't get very far on foot.

Zeke's phone rang again. "Hey, Rhy, what's up?" Zeke listened for a long moment, then said, "Hold on, I need to put you on speaker. Roscoe and Jina need to hear this."

Libby came out of the bedroom, crossing over to join them. He laced his fingers with hers, praying Rhy had called with good news.

Thankfully, Rhy got straight to the point. "Doug and Brady have Charlie Olson in custody."

"Excellent," Zeke said.

"Well, sort of. The guy is claiming he's innocent." Rhy sounded tired. "Brady isn't convinced, and I doubt Doug is either. Unfortunately, Roscoe and Libby have to stay off the grid until they finish interviewing him, which could take a while."

"Understood," Jina said. "We're in Timberland Falls as planned."

"I'll be in touch when I know more." Rhy ended the call. The four of them stared at each other for a long moment.

"Do you think he is innocent?" Libby asked. "Are we wrong about him? Is someone else behind these attacks?"

Roscoe shrugged and sighed. The same uncertainty shrouded Jina's and Zeke's gazes. He didn't want to admit that the only way to know for sure was to wait to see if another member of the cartel showed up to kill them.

CHAPTER TWELVE

Libby felt safe at the Timberland Falls Suites, yet she couldn't help thinking they were no further ahead in uncovering the truth behind these deadly attacks. During the time she'd remained hidden under the overhang, she'd listened incredulously as Charlie claimed he was there to help them. Even having the audacity to encourage them to come out and talk to him. Of course, Roscoe was smart enough to stay quiet. She'd slowly begun inching her way down the embankment to get away from the threat as Jina and Zeke had arrived. Zeke had gone for Roscoe, leaving Jina to help her.

Jina had been amazing, putting herself behind Libby while helping her down the steep embankment. When Libby insisted on waiting for Zeke and Roscoe, Jina agreed but reiterated she was getting out of there the second she heard gunfire. Libby had prayed that Roscoe and Zeke would be able to get away safely, and God had answered her prayers.

But now, she had more questions than ever. Why hadn't

Charlie Olson tried to take them out? Was he innocent? Or was this an elaborate ruse?

She had no idea what to think.

"Flynn and Grayson will be here in five," Zeke announced, looking at his phone. "I sent them the room number of this suite."

"Okay." Roscoe scrubbed his hands over his face, looking as tired as she felt. "We need a plan."

"A plan for what?" Jina asked. "All you have to do is stay off-grid while keeping Libby safe."

"That goes without saying, but it feels like we're missing something," Roscoe said, looking irritable. "Why would Charlie Olson stand at the edge of the Pine Cone parking lot, calling out to me about being there to help when he could have been shooting at us?"

"At the time, I thought he was trying to get us to come out of hiding," Libby said, inserting herself into the conversation.

"I had the same suspicion," Roscoe agreed. "Mostly because discharging his weapon would draw the attention of the restaurant patrons. But as a federal agent, he easily could have gotten away with it."

There was a long silence as the rest of Roscoe's teammates digested that information.

"The guys are here," Zeke said. "Maybe they'll have some ideas."

Libby noticed Jina rolled her eyes. Libby hid a smile. She could only imagine what it must be like to be one of the few female cops on the team.

"We need to wait until Brady and Doug talk to Olson," Jina said as Zeke crossed over to the door. "Guessing isn't going to get us anywhere."

"You're right," Roscoe agreed. "I'm just frustrated."

"Hey, Grayson. Flynn." Zeke opened the door after checking the peephole. "Glad you could join the party."

"It's a little early for a party." Flynn glanced around the spacious suite. "You didn't make coffee?"

"I'll get right on that," Roscoe volunteered. He crossed over to the small kitchenette. "Thanks for bringing the Jeep."

"We also have your computer," Grayson added.

"I'm Libby Hall." She stepped forward to introduce herself. "I've heard a lot about you. And the other members of the team."

"Nice to meet you," Grayson said with an easygoing smile.

"Ditto," Flynn chimed in.

"You guys didn't see anything unusual at the Red Mill Motel?" Roscoe asked as the coffee dripped into the pot.

"Nope. Well, other than Brady Finnegan and Doug Bridges closing in on Charlie Olson." Grayson shrugged. "All in all, that was rather anticlimactic."

"Yeah, we were about to head over to provide backup when the feds took him into custody," Flynn added. "Olson never put up a fight."

"It doesn't make sense that Olson showed up at the Red Mill Motel alone," Roscoe insisted. "Why wouldn't he have brought his cartel buddies as backup? Or if he really was innocent, why not bring a fed or two along for the ride?"

"We did a perimeter search," Grayson said. "If anyone else had been there, there was no sign of them when we arrived."

"I agree that it's strange Olson went to the motel alone," Jina said with a frown. "I guess we'll see what he reveals during his interview."

The coffee finished brewing, so Roscoe filled four cups

and handed them out to his teammates. "I think we should talk to Gabe next, see if he's learned anything from the names we've given him."

"Snake-tattoo guy," Libby said. "I can't remember his name, but I really think he must be involved."

"Pedro Alverez," Roscoe said, when the others looked confused. "He has a snake tattoo around his neck, and Libby saw him near her brother's apartment in Rio Grande City before Tony was arrested. There's already a BOLO for him, though. I assumed Alverez would be with Olson, but he wasn't."

"I'll call Gabe," Zeke offered.

Libby went over to sit on the sofa, feeling a bit overwhelmed by the number of people in the room.

"Are you feeling okay?" Jina asked.

"Fine. Just the usual adrenaline crash after being in danger." She waved a hand. "I don't know how all of you deal with this on a regular basis. Give me a classroom full of seventh graders any day."

Jina visibly shuddered. "No thank you. I'd rather walk into a gunfight than a classroom."

"Gabe doesn't have much on Pedro Alverez yet," Zeke announced. "He confirmed there is a BOLO out on him, but that's all." Zeke's expression turned somber. "The only other news is that the nurse who suffered from the fentanyl exposure died early this morning."

There was a long moment of silence. Libby felt sick at the news. It wasn't her fault, yet she still felt guilty. If she and Roscoe hadn't gone to the hospital to interview Juan Gonzales, that poor man would still be alive.

She buried her head in her hands, fighting back tears.

"Don't, Libby." Roscoe came to sit beside her, looping

his arm around her shoulders. "Don't take the blame for the cartel bringing fentanyl into the hospital."

"Why not?" She wiped her tears. "We shouldn't have been there in the first place."

"We can't see into the future." His tone was annoyingly reasonable. "Although this is a good reminder that we need to know more about John Pollack, the transplant from Houston, Texas."

"I'll boot up the computer," Grayson offered. But before he could move, several phones started buzzing.

"We gotta go," Jina said tersely. "Shooter hostage situation in Greenland."

"That's fine. We're safe here," Roscoe said.

Jina nodded. Before Libby could blink, the four cops bolted from the suite without a second look back. Under normal circumstances, Roscoe would have been heading out with them. Putting his life on the line the way police officers did every single day.

The reality of Roscoe's chosen career hit hard. In the weeks they'd spent together in Rio Grande City, she hadn't known he was a cop. Now she understood that every day a police officer walked out the door could be his or her last.

The danger they faced was sobering. Sure, this situation surrounding her was terrible, but it was also temporary. Or so she hoped. Once they figured out who was behind the attacks, that person would be arrested, and her life would go back to normal.

But Roscoe would simply move on to the next dangerous encounter.

He'd mentioned how much he enjoyed working for Rhy and Joe, raving about the camaraderie with his teammates. Moving from Texas to Wisconsin was one thing. But putting his life in danger on a daily basis was something else.

She couldn't ask him to give up the only job he'd loved.

Yet it wouldn't be easy to live with his being in constant danger either.

THE SUDDEN SILENCE in the suite felt heavy. It wasn't unusual for the team to drop everything to head out to specific calls requiring their expertise.

But it was strange to be sitting there doing nothing while the rest of his team headed out without him.

"I can make more decaf," he offered, rising to his feet.

"No thanks." Libby's voice was strained. "Please excuse me for a moment." She struggled to her feet and quickly slipped into the closest bedroom, closing the door behind her.

He hesitated, obviously knowing she deserved privacy but feeling as if he was missing something.

With a sigh, he crossed to the computer. After the letdown of Charlie Olson's arrest, he needed something to do. Both snake-tattoo guy Pedro Alverez and John Pollack, the cop who had been at Juan Gonzales's bedside were loose ends.

It was tempting to call Gabe, but the current situation with the shooter and hostage situation was a higher priority. He knew Gabe would be digging into the shooter's background while the rest of the team did their best to take control of the situation.

He started with Pollack, remembering how he'd started looking for the guy's social media yesterday, before being interrupted. After a full fifteen minutes of searching, he was disappointed to discover there was no sign of John Pollack from Houston on social media.

The police database? He'd assumed Charlie Olson had found them at the Red Mill Motel through his internet connection to the police computer system. But Olson was in custody and no longer a threat.

Yet Rhy had also told them to stay off-grid.

He tapped his fingers on the keyboard, without logging into the MPD computer system. How long did it take to track an IP address? Was it similar to tracking a cell phone call? Even getting the guy's home address would be a starting point.

Pushing away from the computer, he paced the room. Was it possible Alverez had recruited Libby's brother, Tony, into the cartel?

Snapping his fingers, he turned back to the computer. He'd emailed a copy of his interview notes with Tony to his personal email. Yeah, technically that wasn't allowed, but at the time, he'd needed to write up a report for the DEA and his boss back in San Antonio, so he'd bent the rules.

He wished he'd have thought of it sooner. Maybe reviewing those notes would nudge his memory.

Finding the notes didn't take long, but he glanced at his watch, realizing Libby had been gone for a while. Longer than it would take to use the restroom.

After pulling up his personal email account, he crossed over to listen at her door. Hearing nothing, he hesitated, wondering if she'd decided to take a nap.

"Libby?" He called her name softly, hoping he wouldn't wake her if she was sleeping. "Are you okay?"

There was a long pause, before she replied in a muffled tone, "Fine."

Assuming she was trying to get some rest, he turned back to the computer. Pulling up his notes, he read through Tony Hall's arrest and his initial interview.

"Do you know why you've been taken into custody?"

"You found drugs in my eighteen-wheeler, but I had no idea they were there."

"In your truck and in your apartment."

"What are you talking about?" At this point in the interview, Tony had looked confused for a moment, then crossed his arms over his chest. *"I want an attorney."*

"Okay, that's fine. But any chance you have of getting a lighter sentence will vanish once an attorney gets mixed up in this."

"I want an attorney," Tony had stubbornly repeated. *"Now!"*

"Suit yourself."

The interview had been brief. The rest of his report had outlined how he and DEA Charlie Olson had found the drugs hidden in the door panels and under the seat cushions, along with the photographs of the drugs Roscoe had taken from the day he'd accompanied Libby into Tony's apartment. He hadn't gotten a search warrant for the apartment, which had been a sticking point with the ADA, but he had been invited in by Libby while she took care of Tony's mail. She'd spilled a glass of lemonade, so he'd gone into the only closet the apartment had to get paper towels.

That's where he'd found the boxes. The top flap hadn't been secured, so he'd opened it and was honestly shocked to find the bags of what appeared to be fentanyl.

Sitting back in his seat, he replayed the search of Tony's truck, finding the boxes of drugs and the brief interview, which included his personal notes.

He turned when Libby emerged from the bedroom. He

frowned at her red eyes. "What's wrong? I thought you were fine?"

Avoiding his gaze, she shrugged and stepped closer. It took him a moment to realize she was reading the brief transcription on the screen. With a wince, he minimized the document.

"What if Tony really was innocent?" Her question poked at him since he'd been thinking along those same lines. "What if he was set up and this is about rival cartels trying to get rid of the competition?"

Knowing he needed to tread carefully, he turned to look at her. "Anything is possible, Libby. I admit that when I mentioned the drugs I found in the apartment, Tony looked surprised. But if he really wasn't involved, then why did he agree to work with the feds to testify against the cartel?"

She frowned. "Did you hear that from Tony directly? Or was it through Charlie Olson?"

It was a good point. "Through Olson. Technically, the case fell under federal jurisdiction. I was just . . . helping."

"You mean using me." Her tone was dull and flat. As if she were talking about the price of bread at the grocery store rather than their relationship. "But if Charlie can't be trusted, then that could have been a lie. Which would also explain why Tony had to die in prison. Charlie would not want the word to get out that Tony wasn't really cooperating with the DEA because he didn't know anything about the cartel." Now her green eyes flashed with anger. "You may have arrested the wrong man."

If that was true, he felt sick knowing that his actions had contributed to her brother's death. If it turned out that Tony was innocent, he wasn't sure how Libby would ever forgive him. He swallowed hard and reached for his phone. "I'll text Doug Bridges with your thoughts. It may be something to use during their interview with Olson."

"Charlie isn't going to admit to that," she scoffed. "He's going to keep spouting off about his innocence since he likely realizes there's nothing to prove otherwise."

"We know that Olson helped arrest Pedro Alverez, who was then released from jail." He drummed his fingers on the table, itching to use the computer. How long would this tactical situation keep Gabe busy? He desperately needed information on Pedro Alverez.

The snake-tattoo guy was one of the few leads they had. The rest of the cartel members that had shown up here in Milwaukee had been killed.

He wondered if that fact might help sway either Alverez or John Pollack, if he was also involved, to cooperate.

Prison was better than death.

For most people. Cops were a rare exception. Prisoners often targeted former cops.

After texting Bridges, he set his phone aside, knowing it would take time for the agent to get back to him. He turned back to the computer and went to a well-known search engine to see if he could bring up anything related to cops relocating to Milwaukee.

He remembered that he'd been considered an oddity for moving here from Texas. It wasn't often that people moved from warm states to cold northern ones.

What had Grayson called Texas? Oh yeah, the Wild, Wild West.

To his dismay, Libby pulled a chair over to sit beside him. He wanted to broach the subject of their future, but after their discussion about her brother's possible innocence, this probably wasn't the time.

One of the articles that popped up was done about a year ago, citing the new police chief as being open to accepting applications for police officers from any and all of the fifty states.

"Is that why you came here?" Libby asked.

"No, I came to visit Cam, who as you know is also a cop. He mentioned the tactical team was looking for a new member." He glanced at her. "I applied, never expecting to get the job."

"Hmm." Her noncommittal response nagged at him.

"I told you, I wouldn't have taken the job or moved here if I had known you were pregnant." He hadn't intended to sound so defensive, but it wasn't like he'd gone looking for a job. It had practically fallen into his lap.

"I heard you the first time," Libby said, still looking at the computer screen rather than at him. "And it wouldn't have mattered anyway because I didn't know I was pregnant until six weeks later. You were gone by then."

Yeah, he'd given his notice in San Antonio the moment Rhy had offered him the job here. Partially because he'd liked Rhy and Joe, plus Cam had offered to rent him a room for a reasonable amount.

But more so because he'd felt guilty over the way Libby had lashed out at him in anger over how he'd betrayed her.

His phone vibrated with an incoming text from Bridges. *Call me.*

Gladly, he thought, making the call. Bridges answered almost immediately.

"Please tell me you convinced Olson to cooperate," Roscoe said by way of greeting. He quickly put the call on speaker for Libby to hear this too.

"Nope. But what is all this about suspecting Tony Hall was set up?" Bridges demanded.

Keenly aware of Libby listening to every word, he outlined their theory. "I can send you the notes I took related to the interview with Tony. The highlights are as follows: I was there when the drugs were found stashed in the lining of both doors and beneath the seats. But when I mentioned the drugs we found in his closet, he looked surprised." He glanced at Libby, then added, "At the time, I figured he was just shocked we'd found the stuff at his place. Now I'm not so sure."

"Send me what you have," Bridges demanded.

"One sec." He saved his notes in a new document, then said, "Give me your email address, I'll send it as an attachment."

Bridges gave the information, then said, "You'll find it interesting that Charlie Olson told us the exact same theory. That he originally thought Tony was guilty due to the drugs in the truck and at his apartment, but then began to wonder if the guy was set up by someone else to take the fall."

A warning chill snaked down Roscoe's spine. He did his best to keep his tone matter of fact. "Anything is possible as we both know. But it's just as likely that Olson is doing his best to cover his involvement in all of this. Easy enough to do that by tossing suspicion somewhere else."

"I agree. I specifically asked who would do that to Tony, but he didn't have an answer. And it also doesn't explain why Olson went off-grid only to show up here in Milwaukee."

"Not to mention tracking me and Libby to the Red Mill Motel," Roscoe interjected.

"Right. He claims he had help from the tech team, which is how he found you, but wouldn't go into any more detail related to his thoughts on the case. He refused to say anything more until there is an offer of full immunity on the table," Bridges said with disgust. "That's not happening, so we're at a stalemate."

"A stalemate." Hearing Bridges describe the status of their investigation was downright depressing. And it also indicated Olson was guilty of something, or he wouldn't ask for an offer of full immunity. "Meanwhile, Libby and I are stuck here in a hotel for the foreseeable future."

"I hear you." The DEA agent sounded apologetic. "Trust me, we're still doing everything we can to put the pieces together. Just because Olson isn't talking doesn't mean we're not working the case."

"That reminds me," Roscoe said. "Charlie Olson participated in the arrest of a guy by the name of Pedro Alverez for drug possession with intent to sell. Then the evidence conveniently disappeared, so he was released. The guy has a crude snake tattoo on his neck and lived in the same apartment complex as Tony Hall." He felt Libby's gaze and smiled encouragingly. "Libby remembers seeing the guy outside when she went to Tony's apartment to take care of his mail and stuff while he was on the road. You need to find out from Olson how Alverez's drugs vanished from the evidence room."

"Yeah, I heard about this guy. You're thinking Alverez is the real drug runner for the cartel?" Bridges asked. "Rather than Tony Hall?"

"Why not? He could have put the drugs in Tony's apartment. Someone should talk to the manager to see if Alverez accessed Tony's apartment for any reason. Maybe complaining about a water leak or something like that."

"I like the way you think," Doug said. "I'll put a call in to Charlie's boss, Craig Wilke. He'll be able to assign someone to go talk to the apartment manager."

"A BOLO was issued for Alverez too," he pointed out. "Maybe the same agent could see if Alverez had been around recently." Roscoe believed Alverez was already here in Milwaukee, although proof would be nice.

This case was full of theory, supposition, and conjecture. Other than a handful of dead cartel members and Charlie Olson being in custody, they had nothing concrete to go on.

"Okay, I'll make a few calls," Bridges said. "Maybe I'll have the local police go check in on Alverez. Keep the feds out of it for now."

"Good plan. Oh, there's one more thing. I was hoping to find some information on a Milwaukee cop by the name of John Pollack. He apparently left Houston to relocate here to Milwaukee last year. Claims he followed a girlfriend here."

"Kinda like you did," Bridges said.

"I'm not a suspect," he shot back, irritated with the comparison.

"Don't get testy, I was just saying that two police officers relocating from Texas to Milwaukee is unusual," Bridges said. "Most people move from the cold and snowy winters we have here to the sunbelt states."

"Yeah, yeah," he grumbled. "Don't remind me."

"I'll call you as soon as I have something." Doug wisely changed the subject back to the issue at hand.

"Okay, we'll be waiting." As he ended the call, Libby stood and moved to the sofa as if she needed to put distance between them. He wanted to apologize about his role in arresting Tony but couldn't.

At the time, he'd acted on intel provided to him by the DEA. He couldn't have known the information was wrong or that Olson was dirty.

But it was still difficult to accept that his actions had resulted in Tony's death. And likely a loving relationship with Libby. Oh, he'd insist on being a part of his son or daughter's life, but that wasn't the same thing as being with Libby.

The only woman he'd ever loved.

CHAPTER THIRTEEN

Libby couldn't get the image of her brother's face out of her mind. She hadn't been very sympathetic to his complaints about his hard life in jail. She'd stared stone-faced as he'd complained about the lack of privacy, getting no sleep, and eating bad food. She winced, remembering how she'd roughly told him to deal with it.

For months, she'd convinced herself that Tony had to take responsibility for his actions. That he had chosen to bring drugs across the border for money.

Now she couldn't help but think it was entirely possible that Tony had been as innocent as he'd claimed. That her brother had been set up by someone else and then murdered in his jail cell to keep him from talking.

Reading the brief interview notes on Roscoe's computer had been like a slap to the face. He'd even jotted down his observations regarding the look of surprise on Tony's face when mentioning the drugs that were found in his apartment.

Those drugs had been a setup. Granted, she hadn't known about the additional drugs found in the interior of his eighteen-wheeler, but those had likely been stashed in there without Tony's knowledge too.

All of it had been done to get Tony out of the picture. Why? That part she didn't yet understand.

Battling a flash of anger, she hoped Charlie Olson would spend the rest of his miserable life in prison for what he'd done to her brother.

"Libby . . ." Roscoe's deep voice made her wish things were different. That they really had innocently met in the grocery store rather than the reality of his seeking her out to specifically to get close to Tony.

Why had she fallen for a man who'd lied to her? Even worse, why did she still care so much about him?

"Libby?" He said her name again.

"What?" Her tone was sharp, and she lifted her gaze to his, glaring at him defiantly. She wanted to lash out at him, to make him suffer the way she was.

The baby in her womb kicked, a not-so-subtle reminder that she would have to co-parent this child with Roscoe once this mess was over.

Whether she wanted to or not.

"I'm sorry." His expression was contrite. "I had no way of knowing Charlie Olson was one of the bad guys."

"I know." She hated to admit he was right about that. They still didn't have proof of Charlie's involvement yet either. Yeah, the guy had asked for full immunity, but that could be because he was innocent.

Like Tony.

The entire situation was beyond frustrating. She would have loved to go outside for a walk to clear her head but doubted Roscoe would allow that.

Then again, why not? Olson was in custody, and they had been told to stay off-grid. Taking a walk wouldn't change that. They couldn't be tracked to Timberland Falls by using their disposable phones.

She abruptly stood. "I need some air."

"Wait!" Roscoe shot to his feet too. "You can't go outside. We need to keep our heads down."

"I thought the directive was to stay off-grid." She waved a hand at the computer. "You're logged into work."

"No, that's my personal email. Not work." He leaned over to shut the computer down. "I'm sorry you're upset with me and this situation. I feel terrible you're in the middle of this. But I can't change it either. We need to get through the next twenty-four hours."

"You really think this will be over by tomorrow?"

He grimaced. "Maybe. I'm hoping that once they get through to Charlie Olson's lawyer, he'll cooperate and tell us what he knows."

"And if he doesn't?"

"Someone will find Pedro Alverez, that snake tattoo of his will be easy to spot." He gestured to the sofa. "Let's find something to watch on television. Maybe a movie. I think this hotel has streaming services we can use."

"I don't want to watch a movie with you." The absolute last thing she wanted was to sit beside him on the sofa, all comfy and cozy. She wished now she hadn't kissed him. Mostly because that kiss made it difficult to remember how upset she was with him. "I need to walk. You can come with me or stay here. I don't care." Maybe she was being ridiculously stubborn, but the walls were closing in on her.

Or maybe it was her rioting emotions that had brought on a wave of claustrophobia. Living in Texas meant being out in the sun. It seemed since she'd been here in Wisconsin, she'd been locked away inside for weeks rather than a couple of days.

Especially having Roscoe as her only companion.

With steely determination, she crossed to the door, intending to wrench it open. Roscoe stretched forward to grasp her arm, stopping her in her tracks. She whirled on him, and he instantly let her go, lifting his hands, palms up, in surrender.

"Okay, we'll take a walk," he said, although he was obviously not happy. Too bad for him. He could join her in the *I'm not happy* club. "But seriously, Libby, I'll need you to stay close."

She wished she could tell him to take a long walk off a short pier, but of course, she couldn't. Giving a curt nod, she waited as he pocketed his phone, then secured the weapon in his belt holster.

Seeing the gun gave her pause. Was she being stupid to take a walk outside on a beautiful day? It didn't seem like much to ask. And she had faith in Roscoe's teammates, knowing they would have been on high alert for a tail as they drove from the Red Mill Motel to Timberland Falls.

Especially Jina, who had assigned herself to be Libby's personal protector while Roscoe was preoccupied with Olson.

Maybe after their walk she'd relent to watching a movie. But only if he stayed on the opposite end of the sofa.

"Take a key, just in case we get separated for some reason." He handed her one keycard, while sliding the other into his pocket. He opened the door and swept his gaze over the area to make sure it was safe. Then he stepped back so she could leave first.

They walked past a large indoor pool on the way to the main lobby. There were several families with kids splashing and playing in the water, and it made her conscious again of how they'd work things out after their baby was born.

If she insisted on staying in Texas, Roscoe would relocate there. There was no good reason for her to stay in Rio Grande City. Her dad and her brother were gone. She had her teaching position, but with the shortage of teachers, she knew she could get another job easily enough. And she'd need time off anyway, after giving birth.

"Which way?" Roscoe asked as they stepped out of the lobby to the circle drive outside.

It didn't matter, but she gestured to the left. "I'd like to see some of the trees in the woods behind the hotel. We don't see this much greenery in July back home."

"Okay." He turned to head in that direction. "It's nice there isn't much of a wildfire threat here, compared Texas." He gestured to the gloriously green trees. "If you drive west of the city for an hour, you'll find acres and acres of thick woods. I honestly had no idea Wisconsin had so many small lakes and forest areas."

Just being outside helped ease some of her tension. Yet she also knew this was more than a casual conversation. This was Roscoe's way to hint about their future. She tried to keep an open mind, even though she wasn't feeling very kind toward him. "I didn't know anything about Wisconsin before coming here." She shrugged, knowing she had to be honest. "It's not at all like I imagined."

"It's beautiful here in the summer," he said. "For you, that's an added bonus as you're off school during the best months of the year. Obviously, the winter is cold and snowy. The snow is pretty; I didn't mind that as much as I expected. However, there is a downside to winter. When the temperature dropped to a minus twenty below zero wind chill, my face felt like it would freeze right off my skull."

"That sounds awful." She shivered despite the bright

sunlight dappling through the clouds overhead. Could she live in a place like this? She wasn't sure.

"I agree; that part wasn't great," he admitted. "But being outside on the street in the middle of summer when it's over a hundred degrees for days on end isn't fun either. I've found it's easier to add layers when it's cold than to deal with the relentless heat."

Heat or cold? She wasn't sure which option she liked better. Deep down, she was irritated that she would be forced to make this choice. Was it better to move here, making life easier for Roscoe? Or force him to come with her back home? Summertime was nice, but she'd never done winters like they had here.

The worst part was that Roscoe would do whatever she wanted. No matter how much he liked working for Rhy and the rest of the tactical team, he'd move back to Texas if she told him that she was heading back.

Could she live with that decision?

Splaying a hand over her stomach, she told herself she had a few weeks yet before she'd have to decide.

As they rounded the hotel, she could see a path winding through the trees. "Looks like lots of people walk through there."

"Yeah." His expression turned grim. "I've been here before."

She eyed him warily, sensing the time he'd been here was for work, not leisure. Then she tipped her head back to gaze at the trees. In silence, they followed a short path that led to a large subdivision of new homes, many sporting the same footprint and architecture but in a variety of colors.

"Well, that's disappointing," she murmured with a frown. "The wooded area is just an illusion."

He shrugged. "The hotel is close to the interstate and

likely put the trees up to help provide a sense of privacy. The people owning these houses probably commute to Milwaukee or Waukesha for work. I guess it's impossible to stop civilization from spreading out."

She didn't want to head back inside, but walking through streets lined with large houses on either side wasn't her idea of relaxing either.

With reluctance, she turned, intending to walk the length of the path back to the hotel. Roscoe stopped her, and she frowned, wondering what his problem was. Then she followed his narrowed gaze to a vehicle parked along the side of the street near the front of the obviously newly constructed subdivision.

He tugged her so she was standing behind one of the large trees. His voice was low and tense when he whispered, "Wait."

Wait for what? She could agree the vehicle seemed slightly out of place, but they weren't in the middle of nowhere. The driver of the vehicle could be lost and trying to get his bearings. Or a real estate agent waiting to meet a prospective client.

The events of the past few days had clearly put Roscoe on edge. It was one thing to recognize Charlie Olson outside their motel room. Now he was seeing threats where there weren't any.

Or so she hoped.

She found herself staring at the car too. There was nothing suspicious about it from what she could tell. When there was no movement within the vehicle, Roscoe visibly relaxed, dropping his hand from the butt of his gun. "Sorry. False alarm."

She wanted to snap at him for making her worry but

managed to hold back. No point in yelling at him for being a cop.

That would be like telling him to stop breathing.

She moved forward, wishing there was another route to take as she wasn't ready to go back inside, when Roscoe grabbed her arm again. She turned to glare at him. "What is your problem?"

"Just let me go first." He edged in front of her, taking the lead.

This idea of taking a walk with Roscoe was far from relaxing. Just because he was on edge didn't mean he had to scare the stuffing out of her.

Upon reaching the end of the path leading back out into the open, he stopped again. Then he quickly stepped toward the closest tree, pulling her along.

"Someone's out there," he whispered.

Was this another bout of paranoia? "Hotel guests like us?"

"No, a dark-skinned man." He didn't turn to look at her. "He might have driven the car that is still parked in the subdivision behind us."

Talk about making something out of nothing. Linking a parked car and a man standing near the hotel didn't make sense. She peeked around Roscoe's shoulder to get a look for herself. There was only one man standing there, as if he were waiting for someone.

Maybe he was an employee taking a break. Or something as equally innocuous. But before she could say anything, she noticed the guy lingering near the building pulled a phone from his pocket. He glanced around to make sure no one was nearby before answering it.

Maybe Roscoe's paranoia was rubbing off on her because suddenly the man's actions seemed suspicious.

Roscoe slid his phone from his pocket and thumbed a text. She wasn't sure who he was reaching out to since the team had been called out to a hostage shooter situation.

Whoever he contacted would be too far away to do much good if this guy really was a member of the cartel who'd managed to find them.

Why? Why had she foolishly put her baby in harm's way?

AFTER TEXTING Doug Bridges about their current situation, he reviewed the rather limited options. The guy standing near the side of the hotel with a view of both the driveway coming in from the interstate and the wooded area where they were hiding may not be from the cartel.

But he wasn't willing to take any chances.

He couldn't decide if he was relieved or exasperated at being outside hiding in the small grove of trees rather than inside their hotel suite.

Being tucked in a room with only windows as an escape route wasn't necessarily the best option, as evidenced by Juan Gonzales firing through the door, nearly killing them.

Yet there wasn't much cover out here either. There were plenty of houses in the subdivision, but he and Libby would be out in the open while covering the distance between their current location and the closest property. And that also assumed the people in those homes were home and able to assist.

He didn't think there was someone sitting in the parked car; they'd be roasting inside due to the incessant sunlight beating down on the windows. Yet he had to assume there was a second man somewhere close by. They had two options. Stay and fight while waiting for backup or make a run for the subdivision.

He wasn't fond of either choice. And since he could only see one man so far, he decided to sit tight.

If they managed to get out of there alive, he intended to force the issue of the being able to use the safe house. If not the one in Ravenswood, surely the feds had something similar.

This was getting ridiculous.

"What's the plan?" Libby asked in a hushed whisper.

He didn't turn his gaze from the guy outside the hotel. "Doug or Brady will be here soon. Just stay behind me, okay?"

"Okay." She sounded depressed, but he didn't dare take his attention off the suspect. If he was a suspect. His instincts were screaming at him that normal people didn't stand outside a hotel looking surreptitiously around as if waiting for something.

Or someone.

A dull black and obviously well-used pickup truck rolled toward the hotel. From his position in the trees, he could tell the guy with the phone was waiting for the new arrival.

The odds were spinning out of their favor. He tried to estimate how long it would take for the driver of the truck and the other guy to realize that he and Libby were not inside the suite.

Not nearly long enough for Doug or Brady to arrive.

New plan. If those guys went inside the hotel, he'd take Libby to the subdivision. Surely someone would be home, either working or caring for kids who were off school during the summer break.

If nothing else, they could hide in one of the backyards until the feds arrived.

"Get ready to move," he said in a low voice. "When I say go, we head to the subdivision, understand?"

"Yes." He was grateful she didn't argue.

Unfortunately, he never got a good look at the driver. He must have parked on the other side of the hotel and likely went into the lobby from there, while the guy lingering outside the building continued to stand there, raking his gaze over the area. There was no sign of a snake tattoo on the watcher, but the driver of the pickup could be Pedro Alverez.

For a brief moment, he wondered if he was wrong about this. But then the watcher moved along the side of the hotel. He walked past the indoor pool to the windows beyond.

The windows of their hotel suite? He remembered taking note that the window from the main living space overlooked the small patch of trees. The bedroom on that same side probably did as well.

Oh yeah, these were definitely bad guys. There was no other explanation as to why they'd peer through the windows. He tightened his grip on his weapon but then turned toward Libby. "Let's go."

Without hesitation, Libby ducked out from the tree and hurried along the path. He followed, ears alert for gunfire.

But there was only an eerie silence.

He was not reassured. The two men were likely making sure he and Libby were inside before firing at them. Which meant there wasn't a second to waste. They had to get through the trees and into the subdivision.

Dirt and pine needles helped mask the sound of their footsteps. But suddenly Libby skidded to a stop, darting to the side and dropping to her knees before reaching the clearing.

"What's wrong?" he whispered.

"Look." She waved toward the road leading into the subdivision.

His heart sank when he saw a Caucasian man standing near the black car that had been his first inkling that something wasn't right. Where had he come from? Not from inside the car, it would have been too hot and stifling, but maybe he'd been dropped off there by the black truck to cover the back.

Not good.

The man held a cell phone in his hand, giving Roscoe the impression he was the one in charge. Had he told the other two men to shoot up the hotel suite?

Maybe. If that was the case, it wouldn't take long for the three men to spread out to find them.

The grove of trees wasn't that big. They had five minutes, maybe less, before they'd be found.

They were too far away for him to get a good look at the guy, although from what he could tell, the white dude was older than Charlie Olson. Maybe a colleague? Either someone within the agency or another drug runner.

It didn't matter which.

He pressed himself close to Libby, edging her deeper into the brush.

"You need to stay down and behind me," he whispered. "I'll shoot anyone who gets close."

She gave a jerky nod, her green eyes wide with fear. There was no way to reassure her that she would be fine. Not when they were surrounded and outnumbered, three men with guns to his one.

Assumed guns, as he hadn't spotted a weapon on the

man outside the hotel. He eyed the older white guy, trying to see if he was carrying. Wishing for a good pair of binocs was useless.

He quickly thumbed another text message to Doug.

Hurry, 3 perps, poss armed.

A long ten seconds passed before he got a reply. *Ten min or less.*

This would be over in ten minutes, one way or the other. He slid the phone into his pocket without responding further.

Doug would do his best. He couldn't ask for anything else.

"That guy looks familiar," Libby whispered.

"You've seen him before? At the grocery store?" No doubt the dude had driven up from Texas, the way the other perps had.

Nothing like bringing the gunfight to Milwaukee, he thought sourly.

"I don't know." She sounded uncertain. The guy had a phone to his ear, partially blocking his facial features. "Maybe."

"Doug will be here any minute." He didn't want to lie to her, but she was scared, and he worried about the impact of her stress levels on the baby.

With a nod, she turned back to stare at the older guy.

A noise from behind him had him whirling to pinpoint the sound. Had the two men given up on peering through the hotel room windows?

Were they already closing in on them?

He pulled his weapon, ready to fire at the slightest provocation. Hearing the murmur of voices, he felt certain the two men had spread out to search for them.

"Roscoe! That's my dad!" Libby's excited voice broke into his thoughts.

"Libby, no!" He lunged forward, grabbing her arm in the nick of time. "We can't trust him!"

Their voices must have carried because the older guy at the black car turned to stare in their direction. Then he spoke urgently into the phone as he rounded the front of the vehicle to walk toward them.

Not good. Roscoe tugged Libby harder, pushing her back down to the ground.

"Libby? You'all are safe now," the old man called out. "Come with me, I'll get you out of here. Trust me, I'll explain everything."

Screeching police sirens split the air. The old man paused, then abruptly turned and half ran, half limped back to the car.

Libby turned to look at him with pleading eyes, but he shook his head, willing her to stay put.

There were only a handful of reasons Libby's father would fake his own death.

None of them good.

CHAPTER FOURTEEN

Her father was alive? Libby's heart had filled with joy at knowing she hadn't lost her entire family. She had no idea how her dad had pulled this off, other than her brother, Tony, must have participated in the ruse. After all, Tony had told her he'd handled the identification of their father in the morgue and the subsequent cremation. She had been foolishly naïve to have left everything up to her brother. She'd been devastated at the loss, but that was no excuse.

She should have insisted on seeing her father's body, disfigured face or not.

Yet in the back of her mind, it dawned on her that it was not reassuring that her father had hightailed it out of the Timberland Falls subdivision upon hearing the police sirens. No, if he was here to protect her, he should have stuck around. He should have looked relieved to know that additional law enforcement support was on the way.

Nausea curled in her stomach. Her dad was not one of the good guys. The thought hit hard, especially when realizing how her father had tried to convince her to go along with him. Even worse, she nearly had.

Now she knew why Roscoe had told her to stay put. There was something hinky about her dad showing up here, in Milwaukee. Well, technically Timberland Falls.

Yet she didn't understand how her dad, and whoever else had come along with him, had figured out she was even here.

What in the world was going on? Was her father involved in the cartel? Had her father set her brother up to take the fall for his actions?

Or had father and son, both truck drivers, been working together?

The staccato sound of gunfire interrupted her whirling thoughts. She turned toward Roscoe to find him aiming toward the other end of the path, his attention solely focused on the impending threat. She instinctively melted farther into the brush, making her as small of a target as possible while desperately praying for God to spare them.

The sound of pounding footsteps had her heart lodging in her throat. More bad guys? How many cartel members were here?

"Roscoe! Libby!" She recognized Doug Bridges's voice, but she didn't move until the familiar man with brown hair ran toward them. He was wearing a black vest that identified him as working for the DEA.

"Doug." Roscoe lowered his weapon. "I'm glad to see you."

"Me too." Her voice was breathless as she struggled to her feet. She'd been in a crouch for so long her lower limbs didn't want to work properly.

"I've got you." In a nanosecond, Roscoe lifted her upright. "Hold on to me, okay?"

She'd been so angry with him, but now she leaned gratefully against his strong frame. Maybe she didn't trust him with her heart, but he'd done everything possible to protect her and their baby. Shooting and killing at least two men.

A wave of shame washed over her. This recent shooting was her fault. She'd insisted on going for a walk. If anything had happened to her baby . . .

Tears burned her eyes. She needed to stop letting her emotions mess with her head. Getting mad at Roscoe wasn't worth risking her baby's life. So what if she'd felt claustrophobic? That was better than dead.

"I'm sorry, this is all my fault. I shouldn't have forced the issue . . ." A sob broke free, and suddenly she couldn't hold back a flood of tears. "I'm sorry . . ."

"Hey, don't cry." Roscoe ran a hand down her back. "It's better that we weren't stuck inside the suite. I may not have noticed those guys until it was too late."

He was probably just saying that to make her feel better, yet it worked. She took deep hiccupping breaths, trying to find some semblance of control.

"Guys, plural?" Doug asked. "You hit one bad guy, Brady is back there keeping an eye on him while waiting for the ambulance to arrive, but I didn't see anyone else."

She lifted her head to look at the DEA agent. "You should know that my father is one of them."

Doug's eyebrows levered up, and he cast a questioning glance at Roscoe who nodded and picked up the thread of the story. "Yeah, she was told her dad died of a heart attack, but he is very much alive. He bolted out of here when he heard the sirens, and since I knew there were two other possible suspects on the loose, I didn't dare leave Libby to follow him."

"What's your father's name?" Doug asked.

"George Anthony Hall." Knowing her father was involved with drug runners hurt worse than when she'd suspected Tony. A father should protect their children, not set them up to be killed. Maybe she hadn't been very close to her dad, but it was difficult to comprehend her own father would hate her enough to kill her.

Not just her, but his first and only grandchild. She placed a hand on her belly, doing her best not to throw up.

It was all too much to comprehend. Yet she didn't dare stick her head in the sand and pretend everything would be fine.

No, she needed to do a better job of holding up her end of this deal. And that meant listening to Roscoe and Doug, and anyone else who was trying so hard to keep her safe. She moved away from Roscoe, forcing herself to stand on her own two feet.

"I'd like to know more about Libby's father's involvement, but we need to get you both out of here," Doug said grimly.

"I believe it's my fault they found us," Roscoe said, glancing at her with remorse, before adding, "I logged into my personal email. Whoever Libby's dad has working with him on the inside has some pretty interesting computer tracking skills."

That made her frown. "My dad doesn't know squat about computers so he would definitely need help finding us. But if Charlie Olson is in custody, how is it that these guys are still coming after us?"

"Good question." Doug narrowed his gaze. "It's hard to know if Olson had put all of this in motion before we caught up to him, or if he had others inside the DEA helping him."

"Others? I can't believe there are more DEA agents who are dirty," she protested. "That doesn't make sense. Why would men and women who choose to fight the war on drugs suddenly turn around and play for the wrong team?"

"Money," Roscoe and Doug said at the same time. Then Doug added, "We don't know for sure if there are other agents involved; Olson could have recruited a low-level tech specialist to help him out. The tech specialist could also be under the impression he's working for the good guys."

"Either way, this mess is my fault, and I hope Rhy doesn't kick me off the tactical team for being stupid," Roscoe muttered.

"My brother isn't an idiot," a new voice said. She turned to see a blond-haired man with brown eyes walking toward them. Based on his strong resemblance to Rhy, she knew this must be Brady Finnegan. "And we all make mistakes."

Roscoe looked like he wanted to argue but must have decided they had bigger issues to worry about. He nodded at Brady, who wore an FBI vest. "Thanks to both of you for getting here so quickly. I need access to a safe house. Every hotel and motel we've tried ended up being compromised." He winced. "In truth, it's my fault for using the computer, but I'm running out of options."

"We'll get you in one of our federal safe houses," Doug said. "The only problem is that I need your weapon since you shot a perp."

"No." Roscoe's blunt statement surprised her. "I can't go to a safe house unarmed."

"I'll give you my backup weapon," Brady offered, pulling a small gun from an ankle holster. "I can get another one from Rhy." He flashed a smile. "There's no shortage of backup handguns locked in the safe at the homestead."

Roscoe hesitated. "I'm more comfortable with my service gun." Then he reluctantly handed his gun over to Brady butt first. "I understand, but I only fired in self-defense."

"I know. I heard the two gunshots. From where I was standing, you absolutely fired in self-defense."

The same way Roscoe had back in the City Central Hotel. Horrible to know Roscoe had been forced to shoot two men in the course of two days.

"That's the same gun I used to shoot at Juan Gonzales," Roscoe added. "The local cops want access to that weapon as well."

"Two birds, one gun," was all Brady said.

Taking Brady's weapon, Roscoe looked at it closely, grunted, then stuck it in his holster. "Let's hope I don't have to use it."

She silently echoed his sentiment. Staying close to Roscoe, she waited for Doug Bridges to lead the way back along the path toward the Timberland Falls Suites. Several uniformed police officers were walking the area, while two EMTs were working over a prone figure stretched out on the ground.

"He'll live," Doug said, answering her and Roscoe's unspoken question. "But we won't be able to interview him until he's out of surgery."

"Are they taking him to Trinity Medical Center?" Roscoe asked.

"Yep. All major trauma victims are taken there." Doug stood back and watched as the EMTs lifted the Hispanic man and placed him on the gurney.

"Make sure you don't allow Officer John Pollack to stand guard over him," Roscoe warned. "I still believe he might be involved."

"I heard about that," Brady said. "So far, we haven't found anything suspicious in his background. But I understand your concern. I agree that it's best for Pollack to stay far away from guard duty."

"That will be one of us anyway," an officer said, coming toward them. "This is a Timberland Falls case."

"Actually, it's a federal DEA case," Doug said firmly. "And while we appreciate your help, we'll arrange for someone to keep an eye on our prisoner patient."

The cop snarled. "What is it with you guys bringing your criminal cases out here? You need to keep this kind of stuff in your own jurisdiction."

Doug looked as if he might lash back, but Brady stepped forward. "We understand your concern and take full responsibility for this. I wish we could keep criminals within a specific area, but we can't. Please know how much we appreciate your cooperation."

That was quite the peacemaker speech, Libby thought. Too bad the officers did not look the least bit accommodating.

"We'll still need their statements." The cop jerked his thumb at her and Roscoe.

"Yes, and we have his weapon to match the ballistics," Brady said. "You'll have full access to the gun, but not until later. It's fine for you to take their statements, but it needs to be fast. The danger is still out there."

That gave the cop pause. Clearly, he did not want any more potential gunmen to crawl into their backyard.

The immediate danger was over for now, but Libby knew there were still too many questions without answers.

And the biggest question of all? Why did her own father want to kill her?

EVEN THOUGH BRADY had taken them to his SUV, keeping the engine running so they were comfortable, waiting to give their statements was beyond frustrating. Roscoe understood that if he were the cop on the other end of this, he'd want to know all the details too. These Timberland Falls police officers were just doing their job.

Meanwhile, Libby's father was still at large, working with who knew how many other members of the cartel. Roscoe wasn't sure the reality of the situation had truly struck home for Libby. She'd managed to pull herself together after her meltdown, but he feared the worst was yet to come.

Doug, Brady, and whoever else was helping on this case needed to find George Hall ASAP. Bad enough the guy had tried to lure her away from Roscoe. From this point on, it would be easier for Libby to face her father in the confines of a prison cell.

He had to admit the way her father had faked his death was ingenious. Obviously, her brother, Tony, had been in on the scam. But that only made him wonder if her father was working with Tony to transport drugs.

His mother had been a drug addict, and that was bad. But working with a drug cartel and setting up your own daughter to be killed was far worse. George must be completely heartless.

Roscoe reminded himself it didn't matter. He and Libby were going to survive this. And maybe they could move back to Texas once this was over, not to Rio Grande City, or San Antonio for that matter, but somewhere else.

Anywhere else.

He'd follow Libby's wishes on where she wanted to raise their child.

Finally, an officer he recognized from a previous incident here at the same hotel slid into the seat beside Libby to begin the interview. It only took a few minutes for her to become annoyed.

"I didn't see anyone except my father," Libby insisted. "I was in shock, trying to understand what was happening. I didn't pay attention to the path behind me."

"I'm the one who shot the perp," Roscoe spoke up. "I knew two perps had approached the hotel. Then a short while later, I saw movement through the trees. I stepped to the side just as the guy fired his weapon. I returned fire, hitting him."

The Timberland Falls officer wanted to know more about who these guys were and why they'd come after Roscoe and Libby, but after a few minutes, Doug Bridges cut him off.

"They gave their statements as promised," he said. "If you have more questions down the road, you can contact them through me. This is a DEA case with cartel members from Mexico here in Wisconsin. That's all you need to know."

"But . . ."

"I'm sorry." Doug opened the car door as if he might toss the guy out of the vehicle by force. "That's all I can share. It's time for us to get these victims to safety."

"Fine." The officer looked resigned. "But for the last time, stop bringing your criminals to my backyard."

Roscoe didn't respond, and neither did Doug nor Brady. After a moment of discussion, Doug slid in behind the wheel. "Our safe house is in Ravenswood, not far from the federal office building. Brady is going to follow in his vehicle."

"Good." He knew from previous cases that the federal office building in Ravenswood housed both the DEA and the FBI. Milwaukee wasn't as large as Chicago, New York, or Atlanta, but they still had a decent federal law enforcement presence here.

At the rate things were going, the feds might have to increase their manpower in this area. The Timberland Falls cop was right about the criminals spreading out to previous low crime areas.

After a brief pause, Bridges pulled away from the curb. Roscoe looked back over his shoulder to see Brady behind the wheel of a car behind them.

It felt good to be on the move, but he couldn't relax his tense muscles. He'd made some foolish mistakes, but he still didn't understand how they'd been found. They'd tracked his email here, but Libby had a good point about how that had happened while Charlie Olson was in federal custody.

And how did her father fit into the picture?

"Did you issue a BOLO for George Hall?" he asked.

"Yep." Doug met his gaze in the rearview mirror. "However, don't forget he's faked his death, which means he's likely using a fake ID."

Roscoe inwardly groaned. Of course, it wouldn't be easy to track the guy without knowing his alias.

"You could try my mother's father's name," Libby said. "Timothy R. Perkins."

"We can try, but I'm sure it wouldn't be easy to get an ID on a man who has already died," Doug said.

"He's still alive in a memory care unit," Libby said. "I've tried to visit him, but he only gets upset and angry, so I had to stop going. But it occurs to me that using the name of someone in a facility might be easier than getting a whole new identity."

"Okay. I'll make the call."

As Doug did that, updating the BOLO to include a

possible alias of Timothy R. Perkins, Roscoe glanced at her. "I thought you didn't have any family left?"

She flushed and stared down at her hands. "My grandfather hasn't known me for years. And like I said, the last time I tried to visit him, he lunged at me and tried to choke me. I think he has flashbacks because he served in the armed forces. It's hard to consider him part of my family, when I can't see or communicate with him."

"That must be rough," Roscoe murmured.

"For him more so than me." She looked sad. "I wanted to keep visiting, but then I realized I was doing that for myself so that I would feel better rather than doing what was best for him. The staff at the facility update me regularly and assure me that he remains calm when he's in his usual routine."

He couldn't imagine having to go through that, but it did explain why she hadn't mentioned her grandfather.

Doug's phone rang through the SUV's console, interrupting his thoughts. Roscoe hoped this wasn't more bad news. He wasn't sure how much more Libby could take.

"What's up, Brady?"

"Timberland Falls was able to get video from the front of the hotel. I'll send it to you, so Roscoe can see if this guy looks familiar."

"Was he in a black pickup truck?" Roscoe asked from the back seat. "I saw him drive up but didn't get a good look at his face."

"Yes, we have the truck plates and have issued yet another BOLO," Brady said. "Unfortunately, those plates don't match the vehicle either, so they were likely stolen. Just take a look, see if you recognize him."

"Sure." Roscoe would do whatever he needed to find these guys.

"Anyone behind us?" Doug asked.

"Not yet. So far, so good." Brady ended the call and a moment later, Doug's phone dinged with an incoming text.

Doug handed the phone back to him. He looked at the picture on the screen, then shifted to show it to Libby. "Is this your snake-tattoo guy?"

She stared at the image, then nodded. "Yes. That's him."

"I thought so." He handed the phone back up to Doug who dropped it in the center console cupholder. "Call Brady, let him know the perp is Pedro Alverez. Libby identified him as being outside her brother's apartment building back in Rio Grande City. He has a criminal record for drug trafficking, arrested by Charlie Olson, then let go when the evidence against him disappeared."

Doug made the call, relaying the detailed information to Brady.

"That's excellent news," Brady said. "Thanks for the update."

"Anytime." Roscoe wanted to believe they were one step closer to getting these guys. They had identified Alverez and Libby's father. That was more than they had a few hours ago.

But there was still the nagging sense they were missing something.

"Doug, can you contact the DEA in Texas to find out who Olson has working for him?" Roscoe asked. "Someone is still leaking information, even if they don't realize what they're doing."

"I put a call in to Craig Wilke earlier today." Doug met his gaze in the rearview mirror. "I'll follow up with him after I drop you off at the safe house. Brady is going to stay with you while I continue working the case."

That made sense as the DEA should take the lead on the drug cartel. "Brady is FBI, though, not DEA."

"Yeah, he's doing this as a favor to Rhy." Doug grinned. "You know how those Finnegans like to stick together."

It was on the tip of his tongue to point out he wasn't a Finnegan, but then realized that it didn't matter to Rhy if he was blood or not.

As a member of Rhy's team, he was family.

Resigning his position on the team would be the hardest thing he'd ever do. Well, second to leaving Libby behind in Rio Grande City.

He told himself to get over it. Libby and their child were more important than a job. He didn't doubt he'd be able to find another position in another police precinct. It wouldn't be like here, but it would pay the bills, which was all that mattered.

Libby could decide for herself if she wanted to return to teaching or take a year or two off. He would support her decision either way.

At one point, he'd hoped they might be able to find a way back to the loving relationship they'd shared prior to Tony's arrest.

For now he just wanted Libby to accept his financial and emotional support when it came to raising their child.

When they reached the city limits of Ravenswood, Roscoe looked around curiously. "Where's this safe house?"

"Up ahead," Doug said. "I know it looks like a normal neighborhood, but the white house on the west side of the street is ours, as is the brown one directly across from it. It's worked well in the past to have two houses near each other."

"Good to know," Roscoe said.

When the phone jangled again, Doug pressed a button on his steering wheel. "Yeah, Brady?"

"We have company." Brady's voice was terse. "I'm going to head west to draw the tail away from you. I need you to head east."

"Got it," Doug said. "Call for backup—" His voice was cut off as a crack of gunfire rang out. Doug jerked the wheel as the bullet pierced the center of the windshield.

Then Doug stomped on the brake hard, the seatbelt tightening painfully across Roscoe's shoulder.

Libby let out a cry as she grabbed at the door handle. He prayed her pregnancy wouldn't be impacted by this. "What's happening?"

"Stay down," Doug shouted as he pulled his weapon. But the DEA agent was a second too late.

Libby's father came up on her side of the vehicle, pointing a gun at Libby's head. "Get out! Now! Or I'll kill them all, and this time I won't miss."

"No, Libby, don't . . ."

She ignored Roscoe's plea, unbuckling her seatbelt and then pushing her door open. "Dad, don't shoot. Please, tell me what's going on."

"This ends here." Then the old man's eyes widened in shock as he took note of Libby's pregnant belly. And that split second was all Roscoe needed. He fired through the narrow opening, striking George Anthony Hall in the center of his chest.

CHAPTER FIFTEEN

Libby gaped in horror as her father fell backward beneath the force of the bullet Roscoe fired at him. He dropped the gun to clutch at his chest.

"Dad!" She was about to rush forward, but Roscoe lunged across the seat, grabbing her hand.

"Don't," he said urgently. "Wait for Doug."

She partially ducked behind the half-open door, waiting as Doug slid out from behind the wheel to head over to her father. After a few minutes, he turned to look at her. "I'm sorry, Libby. He's gone."

Her throat tightened with grief, but really, what could she say? Her father had fired at their car, nearly hitting them. Then had threatened to shoot them if she didn't go along with him.

She lowered her head, pressing it against the side of the door. It was difficult to comprehend why her father had turned to a life of crime.

A decision that had cost him his life. For real this time.

"I need to see him." She pushed herself upright, praying her knees wouldn't buckle.

"Wait." Roscoe ran around the back of the car to join her. Then he slid his arm around her waist. "You don't have to do this."

"Yeah. I do." She wasn't making the same mistake as last time. Swallowing hard, she forced herself toward him. Her father's skin was pale and mottled, his eyes were closed. His chest was awash in blood. If she hadn't been there when he'd fired into their car, she wasn't sure she'd have believed him capable of such a cold, callous act of violence.

But he had done this. And worse, he had threatened to kill them all. And for what? Money? Had greed really fueled her father's actions?

Nausea swirled in her belly, and she quickly turned away, taking several deep breaths. Then Roscoe was there, pulling her into his arms and pressing her face into his chest.

"I'm so sorry, Libby."

"It's not your fault," she whispered. Roscoe kept his promise to keep her and their baby safe. She couldn't fault him for that. "He made his choice."

"I think we should get out of here," Doug said, coming over to stand beside them. Lifting her head to look at him, she realized he was glancing around with concern. "I don't like how we were found in this area. Your father shouldn't know anything about the safe house, much less the exact location."

"Call Brady," Roscoe said. "Going to a potentially compromised safe house is not an option."

"I will, but we can't just stand here out in the open," Doug objected. "The car isn't drivable."

"What about the police?" Libby asked. "Surely someone has called the police to report gunfire."

"Maybe, but we can talk to the cops later," Doug said. "Let's move."

Libby glanced at Roscoe. "I'll follow your lead."

He met her gaze, then surprised her by giving her a quick kiss. "Thanks. I'm glad you're not hurt," he said in a low voice. Then he turned to Doug. "Okay, we'll do it your way. But we will keep Libby between us."

"Understood." Doug turned toward the sidewalk. She hurried up to stay behind him, while Roscoe covered her back. She wondered if people in the neighborhood houses were watching them.

The hot July sun beat down on them as they walked the few short blocks to the safe house. She still felt sick to her stomach, either because her baby was hungry or because of how she'd just lost her father for the second time in six months.

Maybe both.

She bumped into Doug when he stopped abruptly. Placing a hand on his back, she was about to apologize when she heard him say, "Craig. What are you doing here?"

Roscoe grasped her shoulders in a tight grip, making her understand something wasn't right. Her sluggish brain tried to make sense of his concern. Who was Craig again? Oh yeah, wasn't he Charlie Olson's boss?

"I've been worried about you," Craig said. She couldn't see over Doug's broad shoulders but sensed the man was standing in front of the safe house. "I heard gunfire, is anyone hurt?"

"We're fine, but why didn't you come and help us out?" Doug asked in a casual tone. "I would have thought you'd have rushed forward to provide backup."

That comment made her realize Doug didn't trust

Craig, and based on the tight grip on her shoulders, Roscoe didn't either.

"I was going to, and I called for backup," Craig said. Even without seeing his face, she could tell the guy was lying through his teeth. "The local cops will be here any minute. Come inside. We'll talk this through."

Roscoe pressed down on her shoulders, so she dropped into a crouch on the ground seconds before Roscoe stepped to the side and fired toward Craig.

"What in the . . ." Craig sputtered as a second burst of gunfire erupted. This time from Doug. She heard a shout of pain, then both Roscoe and Doug were rushing toward the DEA agent with their weapons trained on him.

"Craig Wilke, you're under arrest," Doug said, reaching down to grab his gun.

"I'm hit! You shot me in the shoulder!" Libby heard the rage intermixed with the pain in the DEA agent's voice. "I'll have your badges for this!"

"You have the right to remain silent," Doug said, ignoring the threat. "Anything you say can and will be used against you in a court of law."

Libby slowly rose to her feet, barely listening as Doug continued advising Craig Wilke of his rights. She stumbled toward the safe house that seemed anything but safe. Two men had been shot in a matter of minutes, one of them her own flesh and blood, and she desperately needed to sit down.

"Are you okay?" Roscoe must have sensed her distress because he hurried toward her. His strong arms wrapped around her. "Lean on me, Libby. I'm here for you."

Having little choice as her knees threatened to buckle, she leaned heavily against him. His comforting words resonated deep within. No matter how they'd ended up in this predicament, Roscoe had been the Rock of Gibraltar, holding up his promise to protect her every step of the way.

Selflessly putting his own life on the line. She needed to take his needs into consideration when it came to planning their future. After everything he'd done, she owed him that much.

And more. She wouldn't be here if it wasn't for him.

"Hey, let's get you inside," Roscoe murmured. But before they could make their way to the house, an SUV pulled up beside them.

"Roscoe? What happened?" Brady's concerned face looked at her, then at the front of the safe house where Doug had cuffed Craig Wilke. "Who is that?"

"It's a long story," Roscoe said wearily. "But I think we're finally safe. I'd like to get Libby into the back seat if that's okay with you."

"Of course." Brady put the car in park and unlocked the doors. While she didn't want to leave the comfort of Roscoe's arms, she slid into the back seat. Roscoe climbed in beside her. The blast of cool air was welcome as she settled against the seat cushion.

"What about your tail?" Roscoe asked. "What happened to him?"

Brady grinned. "I called Rhy, and he had some of your teammates meet up with us. Thanks to their expertise, we were able to lead him into a trap. He tried to escape, but we got him." His smile faded. "Zeke and Jina arrested Pedro Alverez, a.k.a. Snake Guy, for having an illegal firearm. They're planning on holding him pending other charges." He nodded at Doug and Craig. "We were hoping you would know more about Alverez's involvement in this."

"Craig Wilke is with the DEA, in a position of authority, and we have reason to believe he's the leak," Roscoe said. "I hate to admit that it's looking as if Charlie Olson might be innocent, but the feds will have to disentangle the truth from the lies. For now, we have one dead perp a few blocks away."

"Yeah, I saw that." Brady turned to look at her. "That man is your father?"

"Yes." It wasn't an easy thing to admit. "He fired at our vehicle, then ordered me out of the car, threatening to kill everyone involved. I—he—" She faltered, then said, "He didn't know I was pregnant. That seemed to throw him for a loop. I'd like to believe he wouldn't have shot and killed me and his only grandchild, but . . ." There was no point in finishing her thought.

Clearly, she hadn't known her father at all.

"I don't think he planned to kill you," Roscoe said, cradling her hand in his. "Otherwise, he would have simply shot through the window. In my opinion, he tried to get you away from the car so he could convince you to go into hiding with him. And that was why your pregnancy had rendered him temporarily speechless." Roscoe held her gaze. "He must have realized that your expecting a baby changed everything. In that moment, he knew you weren't going to drop everything to go away with him as he'd planned."

"You may be right about that." She remembered the look of shock on her father's face. "But I still find it hard to believe that he would have wanted me to go away with him in the first place. It wasn't like we were that close."

"I'm sure he was hoping that being together would help bridge the gap," Roscoe said.

He was trying so hard to make her father seem like a better man than he was. She was grateful for his sweet attempt to console her, but she knew the truth. "My father should have known that I'd never condone illegal activity. Even if I wasn't pregnant, I would never have gone off with him to live off drug money."

Roscoe grimaced, then shrugged. "We don't know for sure what his role was in the organization. Like you said earlier, maybe your father didn't have much of a choice but to go along with Craig Wilke's plan. Either way, I'm sure Doug will work hard to uncover the truth. With everything that has transpired, I think he'll push to have your brother's death reviewed in more detail."

"Absolutely," Doug agreed, joining them. "By the way, nice shooting, Roscoe. I knew I hadn't told Craig the location of the safe house. His showing up was a red flag, and I'm glad you figured that out and took the shot."

"I'm relieved he's alive and able to talk." Roscoe hesitated, then shot her a guilty glance. "I wish I could have done the same for your father, Libby. I wasn't trying to kill him, but he was far too close to you for me to take the risk."

"Don't blame yourself." She shook her head. "It's probably better this way."

The wail of sirens indicated more help was on the way. For the first time in what seemed like eons, she felt safe.

The danger was finally over.

THERE WAS SO much Roscoe wanted to say, but with the local cops swarming the area, this was hardly the time for a personal conversation. He was somewhat relieved that Libby didn't blame him for her father's death, yet he feared the incident could still come between them.

Especially after she had time to think things through.

He regretted killing the guy, but not taking the shot. If

the exact same situation presented itself, he'd do the same thing.

Libby's safety was all that mattered.

For what seemed like the tenth time, Roscoe and Libby had to give the local police their statements about what had transpired. He handed over Brady's backup weapon, feeling naked without the gun.

"I need a doctor," Wilke said in a weak voice.

"You'll get one," Doug said without sympathy. "And you might want to consider cooperating with this investigation. I never gave you this location, and once we dig into your computer, phone, and financial records, we'll have everything we need to send you to prison for the rest of your life."

Wilke stared at him for a long moment, and Roscoe could see the tiny wheels spinning in the guy's mind. Wilke was clearly looking for the best angle to play, and he could barely stand to look at the former fed.

"Okay, I'll give you the leader of the cartel, but I want full immunity and witness protection," Wilke said.

Doug laughed. "No way are you getting off with full immunity. I don't need your help that badly. While you're in surgery, we'll be combing through every one of your personal and business records. By the time that bullet has been removed, we'll have everything we need."

Roscoe had to smile at the flash of panic that crossed Wilke's features.

Yeah, stew on that, Roscoe thought as he turned away. His gaze searched for Libby, and he found her talking to Brady and another local police officer.

"Yes, he is . . . or was my father," she was saying as he joined her. "I'm not surprised he's using the identity of my grandfather, Timothy R. Perkins, but his legal name is or was George Anthony Hall. He threatened to kill everyone in the car if I didn't go with him."

So Libby was right about her father's alias after all. A few minutes of listening to her answering more questions, he'd had enough. "You can follow up with Libby later. She's been through a lot and needs to rest."

The officer glanced at her pregnant belly, then back up at her. "Yeah, okay. That's fine. We'll be in touch."

"You can reach both Officer Roscoe Turner and Libby Hall through me," Brady said, handing over his FBI business card. Then the fed turned to face them. "Rhy has offered to have you stay at the homestead."

"Oh, well, that's up to Libby." He glanced at her questioningly. "We can head back to Cameron's house too. Whatever you'd prefer."

"Maybe Cameron's place would be best," she said with a sigh. "Brady, your family is wonderful, but I'd rather be alone for a little while. If you don't mind."

"That's not a problem," Brady assured her. "But you'll both be invited to family dinner on Sunday."

"We'd love to come," Libby said. "Thank you."

Roscoe didn't response but doubted Rhy would be happy to know he'd be giving his notice. He followed Libby to Brady's SUV, then gave him directions on how to get to his cousin's house.

Thinking of Cameron made Roscoe realize they hadn't spoken since he'd left his cousin a cryptic message warning Cam not to return to the house. That had only been three days ago, but it felt like weeks.

He pulled out his disposable phone, trying to remember his cousin's phone number. After a few minutes, he punched in the numbers.

This time, Cameron answered on the first ring. "Who is this?" His cousin sounded suspicious.

"It's Roscoe. I'm calling from a disposable phone."

"Roscoe! Are you okay? What happened?" Cameron asked with concern. "I was worried sick when you didn't answer any of my calls or text messages. And what's all this about not going to the house because it's not safe?"

"Yeah, sorry about that." He raked his hand through his hair. "It's a long story, but the danger is over, so you can head back to the house at any time."

"What danger?" Cameron wanted to know. "Wait, is this about Libby? That girl from Rio Grande City you mentioned?"

It wasn't a surprise Cam had brought her up since he'd confided in his cousin about how he'd fallen for her, then ruined everything by arresting her brother. "Yeah, she's here. By the way, we're having a baby in early October."

"Are you serious?" Cameron asked. "Or this some sort of joke?"

"No, it's the truth. I wouldn't joke about a baby." Roscoe caught Libby's surprised glance and realized he probably should cut this conversation short. "Cam, I'll fill you in on the rest of the story later. We're heading back to your place now. I just wanted you to know it's safe for you to return to Milwaukee."

"Yeah, we'll need to talk about that. I may not be staying in Milwaukee." Roscoe heard a female voice talking in the background, then Cameron added, "Congrats on having a baby, and you'll want to congratulate us too. Jen and I are getting married."

"That's wonderful news." He wasn't surprised that Cameron had used his week off work to visit Jen and to propose.

"Thanks. We'll talk more later," Cameron said. "I'm just glad to hear your voice."

"Thanks. Same goes." He lowered the phone, very happy for his cousin. The guy was head over heels for Jen.

Then he looked at Libby wishing he could propose to her too. But they had other things to discuss first. *Walk before you run*, he cautioned himself.

He'd made it clear he wanted to be there for their child, but they hadn't ironed out any of the details as to how they'd raise this baby together.

"Is this the place?" Brady's question interrupted his thoughts.

"Yep." Other than the section of the house where the bullets had been removed, the place didn't look like a crime scene. "Thanks, Brady." He got out of the car, heading around to offer Libby a hand. He helped her out, then slammed the door shut.

"I'll be in touch," Brady called through the open passenger window, before slowly backing out of the driveway.

"I'm sorry, but I really need to use the bathroom," Libby said.

"No reason to apologize." He used the keypad to open the garage door. Inside the house, he gestured to the hall. "You remember where it is?"

"Yes, thanks." She disappeared in that direction.

He stood in the living room, waiting for her to finish. When she joined him, he led her to the sofa. "I know you're tired, but there are just a few things I need to say."

She frowned, looking wary. "Like what?"

"I plan to resign from my position with the tactical team." It was harder to say the words than he'd anticipated. "I'll live anywhere you'd like, Libby, except for Rio Grande

City." When it looked like she might argue, he held up his hand. "I don't think there's an opening on their very small police force, and I need to be able to financially support you and the baby. But any other city where you think you can get a teaching job works for me. Just name it and we'll head down to find a place to live."

"Anyplace?" She echoed with a frown.

"Well, anyplace that has a decent-sized police department," he hastened to clarify. "I'm not picky. Anywhere I can get a job will work."

"A decent-sized police department and a school," she said. "Those are your required parameters."

"Yes. Although you don't have to go back to teaching right away if you'd rather not," he said, trying to read her expression. She didn't look as happy at his announcement as he'd hoped. "I'm open to whatever you think is best. Just let me know your thoughts."

She nodded, then said, "I think I'd like to stay here in Milwaukee."

He blinked, frowned, and wondered if he'd heard right. "Milwaukee? I thought you wanted to go back to Texas?"

"I don't remember saying that." She smiled, and the tightness around his chest eased a bit. "Roscoe, I would never ask you to leave a job you obviously love. A job with a boss who cares about you, and me too."

"But you've never spent a winter here," he protested, praying she wouldn't see the flare of excitement in his eyes. Staying in Milwaukee would be great for him, but he worried she'd hate him for it down the road. "It's really cold, especially in January and February. Sometimes March, too, if I'm being honest."

"I know. I'm sure I'll need thick sweaters and socks for

the winter," she agreed. "Not to mention one of those puffy winter coats that make you look like the Michelin man. But if you managed to adapt, I can too."

"Libby, are you absolutely sure?" He searched her gaze for a long moment. "I would feel terrible if you hated it here."

"Roscoe, I could never hate being near you." She edged closer to him on the sofa. "You've saved my life and that of our child."

"That's not a good reason to stay," he quickly interrupted. "I want you to be happy, Libby. And I want to be a part of our baby's life. I'll do whatever it takes, just say the word."

"I thought I already did." She smiled, and added, "I'd like to stay here, Roscoe. With you."

Did she really mean it? His heart wanted to soar, but his brain cautioned him to take it slow and easy. "I love you so much. I fell in love with you when you smiled and teased me about my intent to make my own barbeque sauce while I was in your checkout line at the grocery store."

"Oh, Roscoe. I want to believe that." Tears filled her eyes. "But I just don't know . . ."

"I love you," he repeated. "I know it's going to take time for you to feel the same way. To accept that my love for you is real. I wish more than anything that I hadn't hurt you, Libby. That was never my intent. Unfortunately, I can't change the past. I can only show you how much I care about you as we move forward from here." He paused, then added, "I love you. Please give me the time I need to show you how much."

"Oh, Roscoe." Tears slipped down her cheeks, but she smiled as she brushed them away. "Don't you see? I love you too. That's why I was so hurt by learning you'd arrested Tony. I wouldn't have been so angry and upset if I didn't care." She reached for his hand and pressed it against her rounded belly. "This baby is living proof of our love."

"Yes, it is," he whispered. The baby kicked beneath his palm, making him smile. The miracle of their child was the best thing that had ever happened to him. That and Libby's love. He didn't deserve her, but he wasn't letting her go either. He gently tugged her more fully into his arms, shifting on the sofa so he could cradle her close. "I love you. I promise we'll find a way to make this work."

"I know we will." She kissed his neck, sending a sizzling awareness skipping down his spine. "God brought us here. I know this is exactly where we're supposed to be."

He kissed her, silently agreeing with her statement. When they needed to breathe, he glanced around Cameron's living room. "I wonder if Cameron will sell the house to us."

"What?" Libby pulled back to look up at him. "Why would he do that?"

"Oh, I have a feeling he's relocating to Madison where Jennifer works as a critical care nurse," he said with a smile. "He loves her almost as much as I love you."

She rolled her eyes, then nestled against him. "I love you, and don't take this the wrong way, but I'm really hungry. Can we please eat lunch?"

He laughed, nodded, and kissed her again. "Of course. You already know I'm no expert in the kitchen unless the meal involves barbeque sauce. I can throw together a couple of grilled cheese sandwiches, though, if that works."

"Grilled cheese is great, and I'll make something for dinner." She struggled to her feet. "Teamwork, right?"

"The best kind of teamwork." He headed into the kitchen, determined to spend the rest of his life showing Libby how much he loved her.

Now and forever.

Three weeks later . . .

"The house is yours," Cameron said with a grin. "I hope you guys are happy here." Libby liked Roscoe's cousin; he always seemed to be in a good mood.

"Thanks again," Roscoe said, throwing an arm around Cameron's shoulder. "We can't wait to turn the third bedroom into a nursery for the baby."

Libby couldn't believe how much her life had changed over the past few weeks. Roscoe had gone above and beyond in making her feel at home. He'd gotten her hooked up with Devon's OB doc and had insisted on coming to her appointment.

She'd learned the elementary school just a few blocks away was looking for a new fifth grade teacher. She decided to go back to work even though Roscoe had encouraged her to take time off. But the days were long and lonely without him, and she wanted to do her part in paying some of the mortgage that Roscoe had just taken out to purchase Cameron's house.

"Call me if this lug gets out of line," Cameron teased,

giving her a kiss on the cheek. "I'll head back to whip him into shape."

"Thanks for everything," she murmured. Cameron had given them a fair deal on the house rather than putting it on the market where he might have made more money. Roscoe had mentioned there was no blood bond between the two cousins, yet from what she could tell, Cameron loved him like a brother.

And the feeling was mutual.

Sometimes she felt sad when she thought of her brother and father. Ironically, when she'd gone back to Texas to pack up her things, she'd gone to her dad's place to see what he'd left behind. Most of it was worthless, but she had found an old diary of her mother's. It had turned out to be interesting reading, as her mother had confessed to cheating on her father with another man. The timeframe of the affair made it obvious this unknown guy was her biological father.

It explained why the man she'd believed was her father had kept her at arm's length, never getting close.

And why he'd threatened to kill her.

Doug's investigation was still ongoing, but two days ago when he'd updated her and Roscoe, he had let them know he'd gathered enough evidence to put Craig Wilke behind bars for the rest of his life. Wilke had been working for Ernesto Davion, who happened to be the man in charge of one of the biggest Mexican cartels running drugs over the border. She was horrified to learn her father had been working for Davion and Wilke for years, going as far as to use Tony's truck without his knowledge to continue bringing drugs in from Mexico.

Doug had also found Maria and Josue Gonzales living with Maria's parents in Mexico. They were safe but grief-stricken over losing their husband and father.

Surprisingly, Doug was now convinced that Charlie Olson was innocent and that once Wilke heard about Roscoe being brought in from San Antonio, he'd purposefully set Tony up to take the fall to protect her father.

Tony must have realized that something was going on, as he'd helped her father fake his death. Unfortunately, she'd never know everything that had transpired between father and son.

She had been glad to hear that both Charlie Olson and John Pollack, the police officer from Houston, were not involved in any way.

Cameron waved before sliding into his truck. He'd packed light, leaving most of the furnishings and dishes behind claiming Jennifer already had plenty of stuff at her house.

Roscoe abruptly swept her into his arms, lifting her completely off the ground, pregnant belly and all. "What are you doing?" Her voice came out in a high squeak.

"Carrying you across the threshold," he said. "Hold on, we'll have to go in sideways."

"That tradition is not for buying houses, but for getting married," she pointed out, locking her arms around his neck.

He walked effortlessly through the house. He set her down in the living room, then dropped to one knee. "Speaking of marriage." He opened a small ring box. "Libby, will you please marry me?"

Tears pricked her eyes. Maybe it was partly her hormones, but she was truly touched by his proposal. Over these past few weeks, he'd shown her time and time again how much he cared. There was no reason to worry. She knew with absolute certainty she could trust him with her heart. "Yes. I'd be honored to marry you."

"Good. Because I think our baby needs to grow up

knowing how much her father loves her mother," he said with a grin. It was an ongoing joke—he referred to the baby as a girl, while she referred to it as a boy.

"He will also know how much his mother loves his father," she countered. Roscoe slipped the ring onto her finger, then rose to his feet, drawing her into his arms.

"I love you, Libby."

"I love you too." She kissed him, knowing that Roscoe would always be there for her, no matter what.

And for their family.

I HOPE you enjoyed Roscoe and Libby's story, the fifth book in my Oath of Honor series. Are you ready to read *Jina*? Click here!

I hope you enjoyed Roscoe and Libby's story. I've been having so much fun writing about the members of Rhy Finnegan's tactical team and revisiting the Finnegans and the Callahans. I hope you're enjoying my Oath of Honor series.

I hope you consider reading Jina's story. And of course, I'll be writing about the rest of the team—Zeke, Flynn, and Cassidy—very soon too.

Don't forget, you can purchase eBooks or audiobooks directly from my website, and you will receive a 15% discount by using the code **LauraScott15**.

I adore hearing from my readers! I can be found through my website at https://www.laurascottbooks.com, via Facebook at https://www.facebook.com/LauraScott Books, and Instagram at https://www.instagram.com/lauras cottbooks/. Please take a moment to subscribe to my YouTube channel at youtube.com/@LauraScottBooks-wr1xl?sub_confirmation=1, where you can listen to my audiobooks for free. Also, take a moment to sign up for my monthly newsletter to learn about my new book releases!

All subscribers receive a free novella not available for purchase on any platform plus a bonus epilogue of Elly and Joe's wedding!

Until next time,

Laura Scott

PS Keep reading for a sneak peek of *Jina*!

JINA

Chapter One

Tactical police officer Jina Wheeler threw her gym bag over her shoulder and walked into the crisp autumn night air. There was nothing better than a hard-core sweaty round of kickboxing to end the day.

When Jina had first joined the mixed martial arts gym, she'd been irritated when the guys had instantly hit on her. When flat refusals didn't work, she'd invited them to spar with her. After putting several of them down on the mat in record time, they'd backed off. Now they let her work out in peace.

There was one guy, Cole, whom she saw frequently but who had never once approached her. She only knew his name because Mike, the gym owner, called out to him one day. The two guys were apparently on a first-name basis. Cole was probably married, yet she'd caught him watching her a time or two. Looking wasn't against the law, and maybe he was just curious about how she'd come out on top over the guys.

It didn't matter; she wasn't interested. Okay, she was a little curious about him, but she had no intention of acting on it. Her experience with men wasn't good. During high school, she'd dealt with a creepy stalker, then in college, she'd been attacked and sexually assaulted. On top of that, she and a guy named Jaxon had been friends in high school, but he'd gotten upset when she'd refused to relocate to Nashville with him. She hadn't understood why Jaxon had thought she'd leave her sister behind and after she'd flat out refused, she'd never heard from him again.

Proof that men weren't worth the time or energy it took to find a good one in a sea of losers. Not to mention, most of the guys she met were put off by a woman who could fight and shoot better than they could.

A rueful smile tugged at the corner of her mouth as she headed toward her car, a boxy black Jeep Wrangler. The early September weather was nice enough that she still had the top off, making it easy to toss her gym bag into the back seat. Just because half the members of her tactical team were settling down and getting married didn't mean she planned to follow suit. She was fine on her own 99 percent of the time. She chose to ignore the other 1 percent that she found herself envious of her younger sister Shelly's life.

From somewhere behind her, a car door slammed. She glanced back over her shoulder, cop instincts going on full alert, then relaxed when she saw a pair of headlights flash on. Just someone else leaving the gym.

As she wrenched open her driver's side door, she caught a glimpse of a shadow moving along the side of the building. A man? Adrenaline still zipped through her veins from her strenuous workout, and she quickly reached across the front seat to pull her service weapon from the glove box.

A nanosecond later, the sharp crack of gunfire echoed

through the night. There was no metallic ping of her vehicle being hit. She ducked, her fingers closing around the handle of her gun. In a smooth movement, she held the weapon in a two-handed grip while crouching alongside her Jeep, wishing she had the top on for added cover.

Who was the perp trying to hit? It couldn't be her, unless the guy had terrible aim.

A second crack of gunfire ripped through the night. Okay, now she was getting mad. This guy was going to hurt some innocent bystander if he didn't knock it off.

"Police!" she shouted. "Drop your weapon!"

Listening intently, she heard nothing but silence. Hopefully, Duncan the new second-shift gym manager, would call 911. She peeked up from behind the Jeep, scanning the area next to the building.

Spying a flash of movement, she darted out from behind the car and ran across the parking lot. Pounding footsteps indicated the perp was running away.

No way would she let him escape!

"Stop! Police!" she shouted again as she put on a burst of speed. When she reached the corner of the building, though, she paused, as there was no one in sight.

The gym was located on a mostly empty stretch of road with a long wooded area a few yards behind it. Rushing into the possible line of fire wouldn't be smart, but she really wanted to get this guy.

"Jina? Are you okay?"

She froze at the unknown male voice behind her. Then she whirled to face the new threat. Two perps working together? Wait, that didn't make sense as this one had called her by name.

"Duncan?" She tried to see the bearded man through the darkness. "Is that you?"

"No, my name is Cole. I heard gunfire. I'm hoping Duncan is inside calling the police."

Cole knew her name? For some reason that knocked her off balance. "I'm fine except for the fact the shooter is getting away."

"Let's split up and see if we can grab him." Cole came up to stand beside her, and she noticed he was also carrying a gun. "You head right; I'll go left."

"Got it." She didn't need to be asked twice. Darting across to the woods to the right, she heard Cole doing the same to the left. His movements and actions screamed cop, which shouldn't have been surprising.

Several cops hung out at Mike's MMA gym. Her included.

The woods stretched along the length of the building but weren't deep. She quickly found herself in another parking lot of what appeared to be a strip mall of small businesses. Glancing to her left, she noticed Cole had come out of the woods several yards away as well.

Without saying anything, he waved his gun toward the strip mall. She nodded and headed that way, staying to the right. Upon reaching the back side of the mall, she narrowed her gaze at a parked dark SUV. The lights abruptly blinded her, and the driver hit the gas, going from zero to thirty miles per hour before she could blink.

She wanted to fire at the vehicle but couldn't be certain the driver was their shooter. Until he continued heading straight for her. She was forced to dive to the ground, tucking and rolling to avoid behind hit. Lifting her head, she tried to get the license plate, but the vehicle was already gone.

Swallowing a silent curse—she'd given up swearing since joining Rhy's tactical team—she pushed herself up to her feet just as Cole rushed toward her. "What happened?"

"He tried to run me over." She couldn't help feeling disgusted with her poor performance. "I should have fired first and asked questions later."

"No, you did the right thing," Cole assured her. "Firing at the wrong perp would have required a ton of paperwork."

She couldn't hold back a bark of laughter, because he was right. If she had been wrong about the driver, she would have been stuck in a local police station for the rest of the night. "Yeah, well, I must be losing it because I didn't get the license plate either."

"I don't think there was one, or it was covered in some way." He raked a gaze over her. "You're not hit?"

"No. And I don't think my Jeep was struck either." She turned to head back through the trees to the gym parking lot. It seemed to be taking a while for the local police to respond. "Guess it's a good thing the guy is a lousy shot."

"Yeah." Cole fell into step beside her. "Any idea about who wants to hurt you?"

She shot him a sidelong glance. "As a cop, I make a lot of enemies. But no one specific comes to mind."

"You work out of the Seventh Precinct in Milwaukee, right?" Cole asked.

She narrowed her gaze. "And you know that how?"

"Mike mentioned it," Cole said with a shrug. "I'm a detective with the Peabody police department."

"I figured you were a cop." She didn't like hearing he'd asked around about her. But she wasn't a scared teenager trying to avoid a creepy stalker or a freshman college student fighting off a rapist anymore. She could handle herself in a way she hadn't been able to before.

When they reached the gym building, the wail of sirens

indicated the cops were on the way. Since she couldn't leave, she pulled out her phone and used the flashlight app to scan for shell casings. Cole did the same thing, spreading out from where she was working.

"Found one," she said, crouching down to look at it more closely. "Probably a .38."

"Good eye. And here's the second one." Cole gestured to the casing just three feet away. "Same caliber. Looks like he was moving back when he fired the second time."

"Or he moved closer after missing the first shot." She glanced at him. "Either way, he was pretty far off the mark."

"That's a blessing," Cole said with a nod. "I'm glad no one was hurt." Then he straightened as two uniformed Brookland police officers came toward them. He stepped forward to introduce himself. "I'm Peabody Detective Cole Roberts, and this is Officer Jina . . ." He arched a brow. She was glad Mike hadn't given out her last name.

"Officer Jina Wheeler with MPD," she said. Gesturing toward the ground, she added, "We found two shell casings from the location from where the perp fired at me."

"Maybe you should start at the beginning," the older of the two men said. "Who was shooting at you?"

"I have no idea. Maybe a disgruntled perp I put away at some point." She went on to give her statement as succinctly as possible. To his credit, Cole didn't interrupt. After she'd finished, he added his version of the incident.

"This guy shot at you twice, then tried to run you over?" the younger officer asked.

"Yep. I wish I could give you a plate number, but all I know for sure is that the vehicle was a dark-colored SUV. Not a Jeep, the front grill was different, but maybe a Honda or a Hyundai?" She glanced at Cole for his input.

He nodded. "Pretty sure it was a Honda, and the license plate was either missing or covered."

The cops asked several more questions before letting them go. Jina headed toward her Jeep, then abruptly stopped as Cole joined her.

"Did you need something?" The statement came out more accusatory than she'd intended.

"No. I was just walking you to your car," he answered evenly.

"I'm a cop, Cole." She scowled. "I don't need a babysitter."

"Wasn't volunteering for that role. Just making sure there are no other surprises lurking nearby."

She crossed her arms over her chest. "Thanks for the assist, but I can handle it from here."

He held her gaze for a long moment. The fact that she remembered his eyes were a dark chocolate brown annoyed her. "Suit yourself."

It was on the tip of her tongue to tell him she always did suit herself rather than catering to the whims of others, but he chose that moment to turn to head back to the other side of the parking lot.

Let him go, she told herself sternly. This little interlude was nothing special. He'd backed her up tonight the same way any other cop would have done. The way she would have done if the situation had been reversed.

She took a moment to double-check that no one was hidden inside the Jeep before sliding in behind the wheel. Tucking her weapon under her thigh, she started the engine and drove out of the parking lot. The wind pulled strands of her long blond hair from its ponytail, and she tucked them behind her ear as she covered the distance to her upper-level flat located just five miles away.

The brown and tan two-story brick building was owned by Mr. Glen Gleason, an elderly widower. After a few months of watching him struggle, she'd taken over doing the yard work and snow removal without accepting a break on her rent. As a result, Mr. Gleason hadn't raised her monthly payments in over two years. The arrangement suited her just fine.

Still wondering about the shooter, she pulled into the garage. Mr. Gleason parked on the other side but didn't do a lot of driving except to church and the grocery store. She tucked her weapon into her waistband, grabbed her gym bag, and made her way toward the side entrance that led to her upper-level flat. Mr. Gleason was hard of hearing, so she didn't worry about waking him up at this late hour of midnight.

But when a pair of headlights pierced the darkness out front, she paused, reaching for her gun. If this guy had shown up for round two, she'd enjoy taking him down.

Letting her bag slip to the ground, she darted toward the street. The vehicle abruptly veered away from the curb, tires squealing.

She stared after the disappearing car, noting again the absence of a license plate. Despite her confidence in her abilities, a chill snaked down her spine.

It wasn't good that this guy knew where she lived. The memory of how she'd shot and missed her stalker nearly twelve years ago flashed in her mind.

No way would she miss this time. If this guy showed up again, she'd drop him where he stood without a smidgen of remorse.

CHASING a shooter had not been how Cole had planned to end his night, but he had to admit that meeting Jina was interesting.

He drove to her place, mentally preparing himself for her anger. He'd planned to interview her after their work-out, but the shooter had put a dent in that plan. Chatting with her while cops swarmed the area hadn't been an option either. His only choice was to head out to her place so they could speak in private.

He knew her address and her last name, even though he'd pretended otherwise. He hadn't wanted to open that can of worms in front of the other officers.

She hadn't reacted to his being a Peabody detective, but maybe she'd learned his vocation through Mike. The same way he'd learned about her. At least initially.

Before the cold case had reared its ugly head. Literally.

He pulled into the driveway of the two-story brick building, frowning when he noticed Jina was still outside, holding her weapon in hand. Concerned, he quickly pushed out of the driver's side door. "What's wrong? Did the perp return?"

"What are you doing here?" she asked with a scowl. "How did you find me?"

"Why are you standing there holding your piece?" he countered. "I want to know if that guy showed up again."

She stared at him with deep suspicion for a long minute before gesturing to the street. "Maybe. I noticed a parked car at the curb. The lights flicked on, then the driver peeled away less than a minute before you showed up."

He didn't like the sound of that. "And you have no idea who might be carrying a grudge against you?"

"No. Do you know every perp you put behind bars?

That's an impossible task." Her eyes narrowed. "Now it's your turn. Why are you here?"

He stifled a sigh, realizing she had a right to be concerned. "I wanted to talk to you without an audience."

She arched a brow. "Okay, talk."

It wasn't easy to switch gears, but he had a job to do. And he wasn't about to let a beautiful face distract him. "You know I'm a detective with the Peabody police department."

"Yeah. You mentioned that." She stood her ground, not giving an inch. Obviously, she had no intention of inviting him in for a soft drink.

"I'm working a cold case." He watched her closely, but her expression didn't change. "You're aware of the new subdivision going in on the far west side of the Peabody? Not far from Surrey?"

A flicker of surprise crossed her features, but it was gone in an instant. "No, I wasn't aware of that. I thought Peabody had been subdivided to death."

Interesting turn of phrase, he thought with a cynical smile. Death in the subdivision was exactly why he was here. "Yes, it mostly has. This is the last ten acres of land that's being developed. You know the area, don't you?" He paused, waiting for her to acknowledge that, but she simply stared at him without saying a word. He should have expected her to be well versed about how to respond during a police interview. "Our records show that the Wheeler family owned a sixty-acre farm in Peabody. Elias and Marsha Wheeler were your parents, right?"

"Yes, that's true," she answered without hesitation.

"You and your sister, Shelly, grew up there. Until your parents sold the property. The house was bulldozed, and the land was sold off in ten-acre parcels."

She shrugged. "Yes. Shelly and I grew up there, and my parents did sell the farm after my dad's heart attack. He died two years later, so it turned out to be a good thing for my mom. I'm not sure why that matters now. We haven't lived on the farm in years."

"I'm aware your sister lives in Madison with her husband," he said with a nod. "I plan to talk with her too."

Anger flashed in her eyes. "Why? Shelly is pregnant; there's no reason to upset her. I just told you we haven't lived there in years."

"Eleven years give or take a month," he agreed. "Why would talking to me upset your sister?"

She flushed. "I'm a cop, and you're a detective. I assume some crime has taken place that has brought you here, dredging up the past. Shelly had a miscarriage last year and is in the early months of her pregnancy. I don't want her to be overly upset."

Was there more to her concern? "I promise I won't cause any stress to your sister."

She looked like she wanted to argue but didn't.

After another pause, he decided they'd tap danced enough. "I need to know if you know anything about a male body being buried on the farm."

Something subtle flashed in her eyes. Alarm? Fear? "Are you serious? I hadn't heard anything about that."

"You're sure?"

She lifted her chin. "Yes. I don't know anything about a dead body. Sounds like you believe this man was the victim of a crime." When he nodded without expounding on why that was, she asked, "Do you know anything else about the victim? How old he was? How long he's been buried there?"

He couldn't fault her for asking the same questions he would have. Yet he sensed she was more than a little curious about what had been found. Maybe because she was a cop or because she knew more than she was letting on. "We're waiting for the ME to finish the forensic examination, but his initial assessment based on the degree of decomp of what was left of the clothing is that the body was underground for at least a decade, maybe longer."

This time, she didn't react at all. "Wow, I guess that explains why you're here asking me questions about where I grew up. I'm sorry, but I don't know anything about that. I wish I could help, but I'm sure that poor guy was put there after we moved."

Maybe, maybe not. "You are helping by talking to me." He wondered again why she'd bristled about his interviewing her sister. "I have a few more questions if that's okay."

"I'll do my best." Her smile came across as forced.

"There was a young man who went missing about twelve years ago. Do you remember anything about that?"

"Missing?" She frowned, looking confused. "I don't remember anything about a missing person. Granted, twelve years ago I was only seventeen, but I believe I would have remembered something like that. A missing person would be a hot topic of conversation around town at the time."

He tried to gauge if she was being truthful. She didn't look as if she were hiding anything, but it was dark, and he found it difficult to read nuances in her expression. "The missing man's name was Bradley Crow, and he would have been twenty years old back then." He paused, waiting for a response. When she remained silent, he asked, "Can you tell me if that name sounds familiar?"

"Bradley Crow," she murmured, her brow furrowed.

"No, sorry. That name doesn't sound at all familiar. I attended Peabody High School, and I think I'd remember someone with the last name of Crow."

He'd convinced himself that her path had crossed with Bradley Crow's at one point or another, but maybe not. He tried to give her the benefit of the doubt. "He was probably a few years ahead of you in school." Cole didn't add that Bradley had been a high school dropout working for a local pub owned by his parents before he disappeared. And that his parents hadn't even reported him missing until after he had been missing for a full three months.

He was here to interview Jina, not the other way around.

"Yeah, well, my high school days were a long time ago." She uncrossed her arms as if she were feeling less defensive. "Sorry, I can't help."

He prided himself on his ability to read people, but Jina was doing an admirable job of maintaining her composure while being grilled about a dead body found on her parents' farmland.

Or covering up the truth. It was annoying that he wasn't sure which.

"Do you remember anything strange going on back then?" He searched her gaze in the darkness. "Anything that looking back raises a red flag?"

She looked thoughtful for a moment, then shook her head. "No. Farming wasn't going well for my parents. Like I said, my dad had a heart attack, so the moment I graduated from high school, they sold the property. Some houses were already going in back then, so the land was purchased at a premium. They moved to a smaller house outside of Madison. It wasn't that much longer before my dad died. My mom was a nurse and worked at the health center. I headed off to college, and Shelly finished high school there."

"I see." He'd wondered if her parents had sold the place because of some mishap with Bradley Crow. Maybe the stress of killing a kid who was bothering his beautiful daughters had caused her father's heart attack. But if that was the case, he'd need to come at this from another angle. Jina wasn't giving him anything to go on. "I noticed your mom passed away five years ago."

"Yes. She had pancreatic cancer." Jina's expression reflected her grief and sorrow. "It's just me and Shelly now."

He nodded, and when she didn't say anything more, he decided to let it go. "Well, that's all I have for now, but I may have to stop by to talk to you again."

"I understand," Jina said. "I know how police investigations work."

Yeah, and that was exactly what he was afraid of. "Thanks again. I appreciate your help."

He was about to turn back to his car, when she asked, "How did your vic die?"

He glanced at her over his shoulder. "Why do you ask?"

"Just cop curiosity." Was it his imagination, or did she sound nervous? "You must have found something that indicated he was a victim of a crime."

He hesitated, tempted to simply walk away. But then he surprised himself by saying, "His skull was bashed in."

Her eyes widened with shock that appeared real. Or maybe that was more wishful thinking on his part. "Really? That's awful. I can't believe some poor dead man was found on our old farm property."

Again, he wasn't sure if he was imagining things, but it seemed to him that Jina was relieved by the news.

As Cole slid in behind the wheel of his SUV, he wondered if that was good or bad. Either way, he knew he'd be back to talk to her again.

Very soon.

www.ingramcontent.com/pod-product-compliance
Lightning Source LLC
Chambersburg PA
CBHW070417310726
48977CB00003B/722